By Timothy Harris
KRONSKI/McSMASH
KYD FOR HIRE

AMERICAN Gigolo

TIMOTHY HARRIS

Based on the screenplay by
PAUL SCHRADER

DELACORTE PRESS/NEW YORK

AMERICAN

Gigolo

1

My first day in Los Angeles County Jail they stuck me in a cell with a young guy from Texas who was being held in custody until he could be extradited back to Houston to face a murder charge. His name was Calvin Potts. He'd killed a man with a tire iron in an argument over a glass of spilled beer. He was a little wiry guy with red hair and dreamy eyes set close together in a pale, ferretlike face. His arms and chest were brilliantly tattooed with knives, snakes, nude women, and the words *Death, War, Lucille,* and *Mother.* He liked to talk about cars and the unmentionable things he'd done to Vietcong prisoners of war, like pushing them out of helicopters and making war trophies of their ears. When he wasn't talking about that, he passed the time whistling "Raindrops Keep Fallin' on My Head" and tattooing his knuckles by forcing carbon filings under his skin with the aid of a heated safety pin.

There were two charges of murder against me, one of them involving raping and killing a woman for her jewels and cash. Calvin Potts already knew all about my case from the Los Angeles papers and the newscasts he listened to on his transistor radio.

"Who'd a' thought I'd end up inside with a famous Beverly Hills gigolo?" he kept saying, with a weird, complacent shake of his head. "I just can't believe it. No one'll believe it back in Texas."

He was determined to look on me as a celebrity and he got a big kick every time he heard my name mentioned on the radio. He believed everything they'd said about me: the fortune I'd made, my luxurious life-style, the movie stars I'd known, the thousands of rich women I'd serviced. If he enjoyed the sensational image of me put forth by the media, he was even happier with the criminal flaw in my makeup which had led me to murder a client for her jewels. It never crossed Calvin Potts's mind that I might be innocent, or that my work as a gigolo in reality hardly resembled the glamorous picture offered in the news.

There was not much reality of any kind in that cell with Calvin Potts. He couldn't have been half as stunned at finding himself with me as I was at being locked up with him. I hadn't done what I was accused of and yet everything suggested I'd be spending a majority of the rest of my life behind bars. It was unreal, preposterously unreal, and yet that isn't the right word to describe it at all.

There is nothing unreal about an eight-by-ten prison cell. I'd never experienced anything as claustrophobically choked with reality as that cell, ever.

The one question I kept asking myself was *why*. *Why me?* How could I have gotten into such an awful position?

If I took an honest look at myself, I guess I had to admit my work had tended to make me vulnerable to disaster. Some of what the radio said was true: I was what the Italians call a *marchetta*, which you could translate as an expensive male whore. I made love to women for money, some of them old enough to be my mother. Sometimes I didn't have sex with them at all, just escorted them around and played the part of a sympathetic friend. If they were foreign visitors to Los Angeles, I'd work as their chauffeur and translator and usually end up between the sheets. But that isn't why I'd ended up in prison. The truth is very much stranger and a lot more embarrassing. I did something I'd never done before. Something I'd always considered myself incapable of doing. Something a gigolo, of all people, is never expected or meant to do. I did the one thing which no one will believe possible of someone in my profession.

I fell in love.

2

It all started on a sweltering day in late August. Somewhere above the smog-enveloped city that afternoon, the sun was shining, but at street level, everything was swathed in a yellowish chemical haze. The huge billboards along the Sunset Strip seemed to swim in and out of focus; the pale buildings and shimmering pavements vibrated like mirages in the heat. The air tasted like a nearby tear-gas factory had exploded. From the Strip looking down over the basin of Los Angeles, there was nothing to be seen but a leaden mass of hot air that had hung over the city for so many days, it had almost become a state of mind.

The air conditioning in my leased Mercedes wasn't working. Even driving fast, with the convertible top down, I was bathed in sweat.

When I reached the corner of Sunset and La Brea, I parked in the shade of a tree in front of the International Services Building and wiped my face and hands with a handkerchief. I don't know why it was called the International Services Building. It was just a three-story pink stucco office, like a thousand others that leased space to doctors and lawyers. Most of the top floor was used by a medical consortium except for the corner office facing the Strip. That was occupied by Anne Laughton who, for lack of a better title, was the managing director of the escort agency that employed me. She'd called me in for a meeting that afternoon. She'd been adamant that it couldn't be discussed over the phone, which usually meant that she wanted to argue about money.

It's funny how life likes to give you a warning tap before it drops the boom on you. Looking back, I can see I had one that day and never suspected what quarter the tap came from. As I stepped into the lobby, a blond, emaciated young man came out of the elevator and paused, with trembling hands, to light a cigarette. He could have been handsome, but his face was so thin, it looked almost predatory. I glanced briefly into his eyes. They were dull and hollow, with dark smudges of tired skin beneath them. As I went by him, he caught my arm.

"Julie, baby!" His fatigued face blazed with artificial warmth. "It's me, Teddy. Teddy Lime. You remember me. . . ."

I mumbled some excuse to cover my embarrassment at not having recognized him. I'd seen him in the company of rich women quite a lot when I first started working for Anne Laughton's agency. He'd been one of her big money-makers and I remembered being awed by his good looks and aura of confidence the first time Anne had introduced us. But something had gone badly wrong for Teddy Lime in the interval. I don't recall what we talked about in the lobby that day, just that I ended up lending him fifty dollars. When he took the money, I saw that his hands were polished smooth with dirt, the nails bitten down to the quick. But what struck me most was that he smelled, almost the musty smell of an invalid. The lobby was air-conditioned but his pasty face was running with sweat. He gave off a sweet, rotten aroma of ill health and fear.

Teddy Lime had impressed me two years ago. I was broke then and unemployed, with nothing to my name but a suitcase and a few cartons of books and records. At the time I remembered being amazed that he was younger than me but already one of the most successful gigolos in Los Angeles. I wasn't all that impressed, because I thought the escort agency was only going to be a temporary stopgap for me until I discovered what it was in life I really wanted to do. Still, in those early days I'd used him as a kind of mental model, emulated his taste in clothes, and tried to duplicate his suave, cool way of handling himself.

There wasn't a lot about Teddy Lime left to idolize. After he pocketed the fifty dollars, his lips curled into a nervously disdainful smile.

"I'll have the money for you next week." He shrugged. "That bitch Anne thinks she can put me out of business. I've got friends. I've got clients who love me. Do anything for me. I don't need Anne."

"Sure, Teddy." I gave his shoulder an encouraging pat. He was skin and bone under his jacket.

"They're all bitches, Julian. They'll use you and then they'll sell you out over . . . nothing." He couldn't quite control the whining quaver in his voice. "From now on, I'm strictly free-lance, you know. I mean women like me. *Me.* Not Anne. They're crazy about me. Thanks, man." He gave my hand a limp, damp squeeze. "And don't ever count on that bitch upstairs. First chance she gets she'll send you to the cleaners."

Was that a warning? Was that fate giving a warning knock? But as I went up in the elevator, my main thought was that Anne needed me and not the other way around. I wasn't a Teddy Lime getting strung out and begging favors. If anything, the sight of Teddy only confirmed my own sense of security. Instead of seeing in him a future vision of myself, all I saw was a picture of everything that I would never become.

"You're late, Julian." Anne was slouched behind her desk, her huge pink arms folded, her head thrown back on her shoulders. In her late twenties, she was a sadly obese woman with thick blond hair which she wore in pigtails reaching nearly to her waist. She was what Alice in Wonderland would look like if she had grown up fat and become a Wagnerian opera singer. She was dressed that afternoon in a yellow gingham dress with white ruffles around the collar and short puffed sleeves. Her fingers were loaded with gaudy costume jewelry. Her white-stockinged feet were jammed into flat-heeled, black patent-leather shoes, the kind little girls wear to birthday parties. Her style, if you could call it that, was a sort of grotesque girlishness that was given a sinister turn by her obesity. She had a smooth, almost calflike face with a broad flattened nose and small eyes set wide apart. The impulse behind her appearance, I imagine, was some kind of self-loathing which came out in this monstrous parody of the coquetry of her own sex. She knew she was grotesque dressed as a little girl and got some bitter pleasure from pushing it to the limit.

"I ran into Teddy Lime in the lobby," I said.

"He has no gratitude . . . he has no future." She waved her hand in dismissal. "He has a drug habit and he's washed up. He also smells." She made a face. "How much did you give him?"

"I didn't give him anything."

"Don't lie to me. I don't care what you gave him. I just want to know."

"Fifty dollars."

"That much? You must be doing well, Julian." She studied me for a moment and then slammed open the ledger on her desk. "I've got a job. A woman from Charlottesville. She's flying into town to close a negotiation on her husband's estate."

"Her first time?"

"Who knows? She's meeting with Smith, Silberman, and Hancock in the morning. They want a chauffeur. They want her to have a good time. They wouldn't mind if she was hung over in the morning and feeling guilty as sin. So try and spend the night with her."

"Five hundred dollars and expenses, right?"

Anne looked up from the ledger, nodding.

"Three hundred of it goes to me," I said.

"Oh, Julian, don't start this up again." Her mouth pursed in distaste, and she shoved the ledger away.

I knew it would come to this and I'd already prepared what I was going to say.

"If you want fifty percent, Anne, give the job to one of your younger boys. Hell, get Teddy Lime. He'll give you seventy-five percent."

"It isn't right. You already cut me out of the repeaters. You're overpricing yourself, Julian."

"After four tricks, a client is mine. That's only fair."

"There is nothing fair about it." She tried to suggest a hint of a sob in her throat. "I have no choice."

"You have a choice." I perched on the edge of her desk and smiled. "You can give the job to one of your legion of hungry fags."

"You certainly have a short memory, Julian." She shook her head, a suffering look forming on her face. "You were just a shabby, starving street kid when I took you on. Now I hardly recognize you sometimes. All you seem to care about is money."

"Sentimentality isn't your strong suit, Anne." I walked to the door and turned around. I didn't really give a damn about the money. I just wasn't going to fall for her hypocritical crap about fairness and loyalty when I knew her overriding aim was to screw as much commission out of me as possible. "You ask for as much as the market will bear, Anne. You can't send your other boys on these jobs because they aren't good enough. I'm good enough. That's why I get more."

Normally in an argument with Anne she made sure she got the last word in, even if it was only a final shout of abuse. This time she said nothing. I didn't read the danger signs. Leaving her office, I just thought I'd chalked up a small victory, feeling sure that she secretly respected me more for having been hardnosed than if I'd given in to her.

I remember when I got back to my car I found the seats and windshield littered with yellow handbills announcing the coming end of the world. Lessons on surviving the apocalypse, I read, could be attended at the Oswald Luther Reform Temple on Mariposa Avenue between six and eight on weekday evenings. There was a green Buick parked behind me but there was only a single handbill under its windshield wiper. Whoever had handed out the religious literature must have thought people who drove Mercedes needed extra warning.

It was the muggy afternoon heat and boredom, I suppose, which prompted me to go on from Anne's to the Polo Lounge. Normally I stayed clear of places where I took clients, so it was an out of the ordinary choice. The same thing applies to what I did when I got there. I almost never cruised women in my free time. Outside working assignments I didn't have much interest in straight relationships. Perhaps it was simply that the woman sitting alone in the corner booth was so clearly asking to be picked up.

She was beautiful, but that wasn't what really drew me to her. She had dark blond hair and round, grave brown eyes, a prominent, rather aristocratic nose, and strongly sculpted cheekbones. It was a face divided against itself, and the division extended to the way she was sitting in her booth and how she handled her drink. You could see she didn't like being in the Polo Lounge alone; it threatened her image of herself. She kept her chin tilted up, her face closed into a mask of superior boredom with her surroundings. I watched her hands. The fingers of her left hand drummed nervously on her knee under the table; with her right she made continual small adjustments to the position of the drink in front of her. She didn't taste it. The drink was like an hourglass, measuring the amount of time her pride would let her sit there unaccompanied.

I suppose I enjoyed it, watching her, being able to read the signs. Her way of inducing someone to approach her was to look absurdly and forbiddingly aloof. She was dressed in a cream-colored suit with gray-and-rose piping, wore a white silk scarf, had on gray suede shoes. If she walked you would have heard the discrete rustle of silk; her movements would have released a light cloud of the finest perfume. But it was her mouth that intrigued me; it was full, heavily painted, expressive of an extreme pride. At that moment, alone in a famous bar in the late afternoon, it looked sullen with sensual longing. She was rich, beautiful, and struggling, it appeared to me, with unacknowledged needs.

What should have surprised me most about my interest in her was her age. She was about thirty, well below the age of the women I usually found interesting. But then at the time

I didn't know I was interested. She amused me and off the top of my head I thought I'd try and hustle her.

She'd called the waiter over and I heard her speaking to him in French, asking him to get her some cigarettes. She had a husky, commanding voice but nicely modulated to fall in the pleasing registers.

She watched me cross the room and smiled enquiringly when I stopped at her table. I addressed her in French.

"Excusez-moi, puis-je m'assoir pour un instant? J'ai supris votre conversation. . . ."

"Mais bien sûr." She moved over slightly in the booth.

"Il y a longtemps que je n'ai pas entendu un accent de Marseilles. J'ai été étudiant à l'Université d'Aix-en-Provence." As I smiled at her I wondered why I was telling her about the year I'd spent in France. Generally I made a point of never telling a client anything true about my past. The odd thing was that the truth sounded as unreal to me, as much an invention as the fictions I normally invented to account for my past. You always assume that no matter how many lies you tell, the truth is always there to be returned to if necessary. But I'd reached such a stage of falsification in my daily life that things like my year in Aix-en-Provence no longer held much resonance. I wasn't very real to myself anymore, as if my real self, through constant denial, had shrunk from neglect.

"En fait," she said with casual haughtiness. *"J'ai surtout vécu à Paris."*

That made me smile: her accent was flavored with the vowels of Provence; she was like a midwesterner claiming to have always lived in New York City. Maybe, I suddenly thought, she was as big an imposter as I was. I leaned toward her a little.

"*Je m'appelle Julien Cole.*" Having said that, I felt more in control, Julian Cole not being my real name.

"*Michelle Hasard.*" She inclined her head formally, using her politeness of manner to keep me at a distance. After a moment, she asked me if she could offer me a drink.

"*Avec plaisir.*" I sat back, almost perversely disappointed at how smoothly the cogs were turning. Ordinarily, as a man, I should have offered her the drink. The role-reversal at this early stage was indicative of all that I expected to follow.

She waved the waiter over, a different one, and said in fluent English, "Mr. Cole would like a drink."

"Manhattan," I said, hiding my surprise. "Bourbon Manhattan on ice."

"But you speak English!" she exclaimed.

"I didn't realize you spoke it." I echoed her surprise, looking into her eyes and holding her gaze until she colored faintly.

"But you have no accent at all," she said warmly.

"My mother was French. She came to America when the Nazis invaded. We all spoke French at home when I grew up." That wasn't true but I thought it might sound interesting.

"Really?" She rummaged in her bag for her compact, giving off a rather forced casualness. "My husband is American. I'm waiting for a friend."

That put an end to it right there. I'd been wrong, doubly wrong about her. I'd assumed she didn't speak English. I'd also taken for granted that she was unattached and hoping to get picked up.

"It was nice speaking with you, *Madame Hasard.*" I gave my drink a token sip and started to ease my way out of the booth.

"But where are you going?"

"I think I made a mistake."

"My husband's in New York." She shrugged with a trace of irritation.

"No, I made an even bigger mistake than that."

"What is it?" She was trying to smile through her displeasure. "I've got no special place to go." Saying things like that didn't come easily to her. She was obviously used to being pursued.

"What about the friend you're waiting for?" I said.

"Really, I think you know by now that I'm not waiting for anyone."

"You don't understand."

"Understand what?" Her eyes flashed.

"Understand who I am. What I do." I could feel the smile tightening on my face, a certain panic in my manner. The whole incident was starting to get embarrassing. "Why we can't . . . ah . . ."

"Who are you?" she demanded in a whisper.

"Well, I . . . ah . . . do this for a living."

"Do what?"

"I pick up women."

She stared at me in perfect bewilderment.

"They pay me. It's what I do."

She laughed in my face. It was a completely involuntary laugh of shocked incredulity. Her eyes quickly swept the room to see if we were observed, then she lowered her voice and said, "You mean you came over here and picked me up and now you tell me you only fuck for money?"

It had been a misunderstanding, entirely my fault; all I wanted to do was extricate myself from it as quickly as possible. But as I started to rise, she grabbed my wrist.

"Wait. Tell me. Why did you come on to *me?*"

"I told you. I made a mistake." I tried to get my hand free but she clung on. "I heard you speaking in French and often you meet women from other countries who need translators and escorts and who will, ah, hire you."

"How many languages do you speak?"

"Five."

"And the accents too?"

"Some of them." I finally got free of her grip.

"Plus the international language?"

"Yes."

"And the Polo Lounge is your working premise?"

"That's right," I said.

"You're really something special, aren't you?" she sneered.

"Why get unpleasant?" I shrugged. "You *wanted* me to come over."

She studied me with a strange, cold intentness, making up her mind which way she was going to take it. If she was offended, she was also eager to know what it was about her that had made me pick her out. It was as if she feared she might be manifesting some emotional stigma apparent not only to me but the whole room. I watched her fight it out with herself, the indignation clashing with the inadmissible need to know.

"How much would you have charged me?" She tossed her head.

"As a translator? An escort? A guide?"

"No," she said. "As a straight fuck."

"I don't do that."

"Don't lie. Tell me." She insisted.

"I said I didn't do that."

"Say a number. Just for the heck of it."

"All right, a hundred, maybe fifty bucks." I looked her straight in the eye. "Not much."

"A real bargain," she answered caustically.

This time I pulled myself clear out of the booth. I wasn't going to say anything further, simply turn my back and leave her, but at the last moment I paused and smiled. I remember that smile; there was no anger in it, no bitchiness. I was a good enough actor to get the look on my face I wanted—an expression of faint sadness and surprise.

"You're wrong," I said softly. "It's very easy for women who still have all their beauty to despise the ones who don't. Fifty dollars is sometimes the closest a woman ever comes to having any real physical love. Maybe someday you'll understand that."

It wasn't anything particularly profound or cutting as an exit line but then I didn't see any point in attacking her. I could see how the incident might infuriate a young good-looking woman like her. But then looking back on it, I can also see another motive behind my remark to her. By refusing to respond in kind to her hostility, I'd hoped to shame her and at the same time make her intrigued with me. She was nothing to me and yet somewhere I still wanted her good opinion.

I couldn't help seducing women even when I was walking away from them.

3

I don't remember thinking any further about Michelle Hasard from the moment I walked out of the Polo Lounge. Some people, I suppose, know right from the start, the instant they meet, that they've found what they were looking for. I didn't at all. It was very much business as usual.

That evening I collected the woman from Charlottesville at the airport and drove her to the Beverly-Wilshire Hotel. Her husband had died a few months ago and she was still living under the shadow of his death. She was in her midforties, a trim, dignified woman with faded traces of prettiness in her face and light blue, very melancholy eyes. I concentrated on her eyes. With all women I try to pick out an appealing feature or mannerism. It might be well-shaped hands, a smoothly rounded hip, or a look that crosses a face in repose. It doesn't have to be anything conventionally beautiful. Often it's just the opposite: some nervous lack of confidence or sign of vulnerability in them which wins me over. Whatever, I need this sense of their humanity and their suffering in order to desire them. Without it, I don't find them attractive.

They say good actors can cry at will in front of the film

cameras simply by conjuring unhappy memories. I suppose I work in much the same way. I find some feature or aspect in the woman which gives me a feeling of melancholy and that generally leads to arousal.

It's, of course, a solitary, artificial act on my part. Still, like real Method acting, it sometimes almost borders on a kind of truth.

I have to pity them before I can make love to them, which is to say, as my analyst always tells me, I have to be in complete control.

Mrs. Browning, the woman from Charlottesville, didn't really know what the setup was, but I had the feeling she liked me and was too shy to do anything about it. There were flowers and a magnum of Dom Perignon on ice waiting in her suite when we arrived. While she unpacked, I opened the champagne and brought her a glass. She told me she'd be pleased if I'd have a glass with her. She seemed rather sad and distracted. I sensed the trip to Los Angeles and her husband's death were upsetting her and what she really wanted to do was break down and cry. Instead of skirting the subject, I encouraged her to talk about it, and pretty soon she was crying into her champagne.

By then I really did feel sorry for her. She was sitting on the edge of the bed, her mascara and face powder washing away with the tears, babbling about how embarrassed she was to be carrying on like that in front of a stranger. I took the glass from her hand and sat down next to her. I closed one hand around the back of her neck and with the other stroked her hair. At first the muscles in her neck went rigid, then they softened and she sighed with relief. For the moment she wanted to be soothed and mothered. I cradled her shoulders and rubbed her head like a child and then gently, with the same motions, massaged her back, descending until my hand was probing the stiffened tendons at the base of her spine. She was breathing shallowly, her face hidden in my chest, her body rigid with tension.

I was a total stranger, a young chauffeur, and she was in mourning. I was sure those were the kind of arguments going through her mind as she let me caress her. I didn't want her to reflect. I kissed her neck and pressed my hand down between her buttocks. When she didn't resist, I slid my hand all the way until my fingers were inside her. She was completely wet; she had been wet the whole time I was stroking her head.

After that I didn't worry any more. I didn't even bother to entirely undress her or myself. I unrolled her underpants and slipped out of my trousers. I was only semierect. I cupped her face in my hands and kissed her lips and after a moment her eyes opened: light blue melancholy eyes, glazed-over and distant. I kept my attention fixed on them, communing with them, loving them, and I felt myself hardening.

Once I was inside Mrs. Browning, I just worked. The physical pleasure was mainly hers; mine was more mental, a pleasure of the will controlling my movements, an intellectual curiosity as I sought the rhythm and motion that her body wanted.

I might as well say that in that department my sex life was pretty uninteresting; it was very hard for me to have orgasms and when I came, it was rarely the kind of deep-reaching sensation men are meant to experience. In fact, it was usually an almost half-painful release which left me swollen and bafflingly depressed. Clinically my condition was known as satyriasis, the male form of nymphomania. It meant I was always ready for sex, always wanted it, but it never really could take me over or change how I felt.

That's the naked truth behind Julian Cole, Beverly Hills Casanova, as one newspaper has called me. Sure, I could service anyone at just about any time for as long as was required, the reason being that I could hardly ever come, and even when I did come, it was superficial, leaving most of my sexual energy still unrelieved.

My analyst insists I must secretly resent women because of my condition. Mrs. Browning, for instance, had me inside her for an hour, and the whole time I was as rock-hard as when I first entered her. In that hour she unraveled. That's the only word I can think of to describe the changes she went through. With every successive orgasm, she unlocked more of herself, opened up more deeply buried regions of pleasure. Her blood was pumping through sets of muscles she'd forgotten she had, enlivening nerves that had been neglected and frozen for years. She didn't have to grab at her pleasure for fear it was going to be snatched away.

I wasn't about to resent her. If I couldn't let myself go as she could, at least I could be proud that I was the means to her pleasure. Afterwards, when she told me that for the last ten years of her life, she'd given up hope of ever feeling anything again, I thought I'd done a good thing.

Maybe my pity for women is disguised pity for myself. Maybe I'm like a reformed alcoholic who enjoys watching other people drink. That is nothing much to be proud of, but it's a higher human reaction than simple resentment.

Mrs. Browning ended up in a wild delirious coma of gratitude. She knew I hadn't come and was determined to give me an orgasm. She wouldn't let me go. Nothing would stop her from going down on me. Vanity and a desire to please drove her into a very studied, artful blowjob, an educated, thoughtful, imaginative blowjob. I understood what she was trying to do; it was genuinely an act of generosity for my benefit but it was wasted. My prick was so hard it ached, but I wasn't any nearer coming. After about a quarter of an hour I made her stop, lamely explaining that my bladder was full, which made it hard for me to come.

You can rarely fool people in bed. A part of them can be tricked, or distracted, but something in them knows and registers any holding back. So you have a drink, or smoke a cigarette, or talk about something else. You draw a cover over the emptiness. She knew and I knew that what we'd done hadn't been together. She knew I was a professional; no matter how thoughtful or kind I was to her, she sensed it was a technique more than a personal attraction. Over dinner in her suite, that knowledge gave our conversation a certain forced animation; we were careful never to let long silences develop. We ate lavishly and drank too much wine, and she insisted on cognac after the meal. She downed two large snifters and started reminiscing about her husband again. She told me she had a son my age who was in his final year of medical school in Boston. She started to show me a picture and then her face crumpled and she let her purse drop to the floor. She bowed her head, her shoulders trembling. In a muffled voice she told me she wasn't used to drinking so much and didn't feel very well.

"You don't have to spend the night with me," she said.

"But I want to spend the night with you," I said warmly.

"Please don't say anything." She got up from the table and went into the bedroom and shut the door. I heard the key turning in the lock and then the sound of her crying above the roar of running water.

I'd given her something but of course I'd also depressed the hell out of her. You always hurt the nicest ones; in the end you always sadden them.

*   *   *

I drifted through the lobby, past the guests and bellhops, unaccountably depressed by the scene with Mrs. Browning. I thought maybe I was getting too old for the work, although twenty-five wasn't a very advanced age. Lately, the letdown after a job seemed more pronounced than it used to be. I'd had quite a bit to drink but I felt boringly sober. I'd have gone to a bar but I knew it wouldn't do any good in this mood. Or I could go home and dose myself with sleeping pills but the prospect depressed me even more than the idea of a bar. What was the matter with me? I could go anywhere and do anything I wanted. The years of hard work had paid off: I was at the top of my profession, accepted everywhere in Los Angeles. I'd become a successful part of that wealthy, sophisticated milieu that I'd so wanted to belong to as a child. No one would ever guess how poor and illiterate my parents had been, or know anything about my shabby childhood, the years of living in foster homes, my lack of formal education. I'd taught myself well, absorbed the mannerisms of the rich, and improved my mind. Yes, I thought, but you never imagined it like this. There was always something else you wanted to do, this was to be only a preparation, a stepping-stone for that other thing. *But what thing?*

With an uneasy feeling I realized I'd had this same conversation with myself for many months, almost always after being with a client. I always shook it off and it always returned. It wasn't just a passing mood anymore; it was becoming a chronic part of me and I was learning to live with it. I was *accepting* it. That's what scared me. My life was going in circles and the circles were getting smaller and smaller, like a whirlpool, and I didn't seem able to break out of it.

The restless, uneasy mood was still with me when I woke

up in the morning in my hotel room. Over breakfast I listened to a Berlitz *Learn Swedish* tape. Anne Laughton had arranged a job for me later in the month that would involve escorting the wife of a wealthy Swedish industrialist around Los Angeles. The tape would ask a question and I would say the response aloud in Swedish through a mouthful of toast. I practiced for about an hour and then did fifteen minutes of isometric exercises. After that I put on a Verdi requiem and went through my yoga exercises. It wasn't that I was particularly obsessed with my body; it was more a hangover from my past. When I was younger I was in a desperate rush to improve myself by every possible means. I read constantly, studied languages, lifted weights, made lists of the classical pieces I wanted to learn to play, memorized the names of wines, learned who made the best shoes, jewelry, suits. I was like an actor preparing himself for an arduous role. I wanted to have the best taste in everything.

Standing on my head that morning, I seriously wondered if it had been worth all the effort. Every minute of my day had to be filled with some purposeful activity, but in aid of what? What was I in training for? My room was filled with literature, art books, and records. There were illustrated charts all over the walls tracing the history of antique French furniture, Chinese jade, English porcelain, European painting. I'd made myself knowledgeable in these areas, but did any of them really touch me? I didn't even enjoy Verdi anymore. I didn't even know if I'd *ever* enjoyed Verdi, or particularly cared about Louis Quinze furniture either.

So that's the mood I was in when Leroy, the spade pimp, called: upside down and having an identity crisis.

"Julian, baby." His hoarse, childishly sweet voice had a whine in it like the squeak in a hinge. "I hate to bug you like this, but you gotta help me out."

I didn't exactly jump at the prospect of doing anything for Leroy. He was a dapper black faggot who ran a mainly gay escort service out of Beverly Hills and did a thriving business dealing cocaine on the side. I'd gone on a few gigs for him in my first weeks in Hollywood but I'd never felt comfortable around him. He only made it with white boys and like a lot of black men who only go with white women, part of Leroy's motive, I felt, was to even some old racial scores.

"I had this Beverly Hills trick set up for Joey tonight," he said. "And he's split on me."

"I can't do it, Leroy," I lied. "I got a gig this afternoon."

"Baby, it's a one-hour job. You ain't even gonna have to take your clothes off. Some bitch wants her ass paddled, that's all."

"Who needs that weirdness, man. I can't make that scene."

"Hey, this is me, Leroy, talking. I ain't setting you up for no heavy trick. Five hundred bucks just to give her a light spanking."

Everything told me to turn it down. The job wasn't my style and I'd long outgrown working for Leroy. I should have flatly refused him but I didn't. He'd had a crush on me when I first worked for him which he'd publicized by telling everyone and loudly drowning his sorrows in the gay bars. He was one of those gays who indulged himself in hopeless infatuations with men who would never reciprocate his advances. It had been something of a public humiliation for him when I left him to work for Anne. So, thinking to spare his feelings, I didn't tell him I didn't want the gig but instead asked for four of the five hundred dollars.

"Fuck that, Jack. You think I'm in the charity business?"

"Well, that's it, Leroy. You'd make out better getting someone else."

"Shit fuck!" he cried. When it got down to money, Leroy's vocabulary dropped straight back into the ghetto. "I can't get no one else and you know it. Man, why you doing this to me? There ain't a hustler in this town gets eighty percent and you know it."

"Sorry, Leroy."

"You sorry?" he said. "I remember when you come to me. You didn't have shit to your name. All my boys did what I said except you. You wouldn't let anyone touch you. You don't remember what I did for you? I sent you out with nothing but old fairies who just wanted to hold your hand. Man, I dug you. I made you some jack, brother. I protected you."

"Jesus Christ, Leroy, I did three gigs for you two years ago and you act like you brought me up. Listen, I don't want the trick. It isn't the money."

"Oh, man, don't say that. Oh, Julian, honey, don't let me hear that. You don't turn down business. Ain't no one going to want you, you start turning down tricks. That's a bad sign. That's the sin of pride. I seen too many hustlers go down that way, pricing themselves right out of the market."

"That's what Anne told me."

"Listen to her. She knows what she's talking about."

"If I listened to her, I wouldn't even be talking to you."

"Take three hundred, brother. I don't want to beg."

"Okay." I sighed. "Call back and give my service the information. I'm bad with details."

4

If the job had felt wrong from the start, the conviction only deepened when I got Leroy's message on my answering service. He had said it was a Beverly Hills woman, but my instructions were to go to a motel in East Hollywood and ask for a Mr. Ryman. The more I considered it, the screwier it sounded. For a start the price was way too high for the kind of job he'd described. Leroy hadn't mentioned anything to me about a man. The location was even more suspicious. Why wasn't I going to the client's home, or at least a decent hotel in a better part of town? People who could afford five hundred dollars for an hour's sex didn't rent motel rooms in the seamiest section of Hollywood.

So you couldn't say I didn't have fair warning. I could have been deaf, dumb, and blind and known that no good would come of it.

Night had already fallen by the time I got to Hollywood Boulevard. The day's smog still hung in the air but the city's blazing lights had turned it a radiant gray. There were no stars, or moon, or clouds, no sense of the great western sky opening up overhead. The city was roofed in by the low, artificially illuminated cover of smog which seemed to press down with an unhealthy, glowing light of its own. The evening traffic moved in a slow parade past the junk-food stands, the sex shops, the all-night cinemas, and strip shows. Strange varieties of night life—glitter queens, ragpickers, tattooed sailors, pimps, adolescent hustlers made their moves in the steamy, poisoned air. There was a barbarous sensuality, an almost Roman or Asiatic feel to the city on such a sweltering summer night. Everywhere you were conscious of bare, sun-burned skin, oiled bodies, the flash of haunches and breasts, the smell of frying food mingled with the sound of electric music blaring out of the bars and massage parlors. In the distance, above the bedlam of traffic, voices, and music, you could just hear the wail of police sirens floating like a refrain from far across the city.

I found the motel on a corner east of Hollywood and Normandie. It was called the Taj Mahal and it was the kind of seedy dump where you'd expect someone like Philip Marlowe to find a dead blond in the shower. The front of the building was a flattened, one-dimensional version of the Taj Mahal in rough, dirty-white stucco, with wire screens over the windows, and a green neon sign over the entrance that flashed only three letters.

In the lobby an old Japanese man sat behind the reception desk, his face glued to a rerun of *Casablanca* on a portable television set. He had a narrow bald head the color of soiled ivory and eyes gone vague and opaque with cataracts.

"I'm here to see Mr. Ryman," I said.

"Room two-oh-three." He stared at me but it was impossible to tell how much he could actually see; his eyes looked like cloudy, decomposing crystals, giving off some last radiance before death closed them. "He wait for you," the old man said, and turned back to his TV.

I crossed the lobby to the antique iron-grill elevator. The

place smelled of disinfectant and unemptied ashtrays. Going up, the draft moved the air in the elevator shaft, wafting up smells of soot and engine oil.

There's not much point in reflecting that I almost pushed the ground floor button, almost took the elevator back down, almost walked out; I didn't.

Room 203 was at the end of a narrow, dimly lit hall. I remember there were moths fluttering around the lamps whose glass bowls were already filled with the dark bodies of dead insects. The window at the end of the hall was open on a ventilator shaft that must have led to the kitchen. I could smell coffee and grease and fried fish.

Voices were coming through the door of 203. I heard a woman sigh querulously, "I don't want *another* one." Then another voice, a man's, said breathlessly, "I just want you to feel right this time."

When I knocked the voices stopped.

A middle-aged man in a white satin dressing gown answered the door. He had a long face, a very thin-lipped mouth, and a high-domed forehead. His skin was shiny and minutely wrinkled, almost varnished looking. Thick-lensed spectacles enlarged his eyes and gave them a slightly disturbing goldfish-bowl quality. His silver hair was slicked back from his forehead and he smelled strongly of a lilac-scented cologne.

"Julian Cole?" he said with a wheeze in his voice.

"Yes."

"Please come in. This way . . ." He had trouble breathing and seemed to be trying to catch his breath. I followed him down a short passage into a shabbily decorated room. A woman in a flowered black silk kimono was lying curled up on the bed. A young woman with a vacant, carefully painted face. She was dark haired, deeply tanned, with large, heavy-lidded blue eyes which seemed to hardly register me. Her mouth hung open a little. Just looking at her hair, her nails, her robe, and accessories I could tell she lived in Beverly Hills. She had that high-glossed finish that comes from an incessant preoccupation with one's physical appearance. I felt Ryman wheezing behind me.

"I think someone made a mistake." I turned around. "I don't do couples."

"Let me get you a drink." He motioned toward a side table liberally stacked with good liquor, a silver ice bucket, a cocktail shaker, and crystal glasses. It looked thoroughly out of place in the crummy room.

"No thanks. Look, Leroy never told me . . ."

"No, no, you don't understand. It's just my wife. Julie. Not me." He wiped his forehead with a hankie and then patted his lips. "Just her."

"Hello." I smiled at his wife. She moved her lips and said hello back in an almost inaudible whisper, and then failed to suppress a yawn. I had a feeling she was doped up to the eyeballs.

"But I can watch." Ryman cleared his throat.

"That's all?" I said. "You just want to watch?"

"That would be all." He coughed and wiped his lips again. "And . . . and . . . afterwards I like to talk. That too."

If he was a voyeur it didn't worry me so much since they're usually harmless nonviolent types. I tried to put him out of my mind. I sat down on the edge of the bed and took his wife's hand. It was soft and damp. A humid, lovely smell came from her body. I didn't know how old she was— perhaps in her early twenties, though her slightly puffed eyes and slack mouth made her look younger. I slipped out of my shoes and unbuttoned my shirt which she helped me off with, moving very slowly and languidly, like someone in a dream. I was someone else to her. I could tell that at once. Some powerful fantasy was at work in her mind which she was being very careful not to disrupt.

I laid my trousers on the bedside table next to a tin bowling trophy which had been converted into a lamp. I was vaguely aware of Ryman somewhere behind me: the rustle of his shallow breathing, the clink of ice in a glass. I didn't want to think of him. I spoke softly to his wife as if she were the only person in the room, unloosening her robe, and brushing my lips over her stomach. I kissed my way upwards to her full, bronzed breasts, cupping them lightly, darting my tongue against their hardened nipples. Her hands closed round my head and pressed me tighter. She whispered in a distant voice, "Bite me. Bite me hard. I want you to hurt me."

It didn't really turn me on but I tried to do as she wanted, squeezing harder and taking little bites at her nipples. After awhile she reached between my legs. She cupped my balls and delicately squeezed them and then ran her fingernails lightly along the length of my erection.

"Harder. Bite me harder."

I tried to do what she wanted, but the whole time my mind was disassociated from the act. I kept wondering why this obviously wealthy couple had chosen the Taj Mahal to stage their sex game. Was a cheap motel room some vital ingredient in their fantasy? And whose fantasy was it? His or hers?

"Now," she whispered. "Fuck me now."

I started to climb on top of her when Ryman suddenly wheezed behind me. "From the back. It has to be done from the back."

I looked at his wife but her eyes were drowsy, empty

pools that showed no reaction. I slipped my hand under her body and flipped her over on her stomach. What I saw made me catch my breath. The backs of her thighs and buttocks were ribbed with bruised welts and scratches. I stroked my hand between her legs but she was completely and bafflingly dry. She guided my fingers to her ass which was already richly lubricated with oil. Undulating beneath me, she spread her buttocks wide apart with her hands and offered herself.

"Fuck her in the ass," Ryman whispered.

I was so big I was afraid I'd hurt her but when I tried to inch my way in slowly she corkscrewed up against me and took almost all of it in two gliding plunges. "Now hard," she gasped. "Fuck me in the ass. Fuck me in the ass." She repeated it like a litany, with unreal passion, as if it were a prerehearsed element which she or her husband had to hear to get off. I tried to touch her clitoris but she was still utterly dry. She had very strangely wired erogenous zones and they all seemed to be tuned in to physical pain. As I stroked in and out of her, she clawed her own buttocks, raking herself with her scarlet manicured nails and sobbing that it hurt.

"Now slap her," Ryman cried, "slap that cunt."

I didn't know what he was doing behind me. I didn't want to look. His voice was strident, alive with a gloating hysteria. I didn't strike her but he shouted again and she started begging me to hit her as well. She was clawing herself so violently she was drawing blood which was starting to get on my thighs and stomach. I clipped her lightly on the back of the neck and then sort of slapped her arms. It was an awkward position to hit anyone—human beings had been intended to do something else in it—and I felt very dejected by it all. It wasn't nearly violent enough for either of them. They were both urging me to hurt her more. I wanted to get it over with. I just wanted out of there. The blood, the neurotic hysteria, the incessant commands and instructions were getting on my nerves. I slapped her hard on the shoulder and I felt her rectum convulse and tighten. I slugged her again and she accelerated into a wild burning anal orgasm, emitting sobbing cries that seemed as full of pain as of pleasure.

And then it was over. She jerked herself free, and turned on her side, hugging her arms and burying her face in the pillow. I propped myself up on my elbow and met Ryman's gaze. He was slumped in an armchair, with his legs apart and a handkerchief pressed to his groin. His eyes had a shocked, insane radiance, unblinking as a lizard. Dry spit flecked the corners of his mouth; his breath came in fierce, shallow pants.

His wife stirred beside me and then went into the bathroom where I heard water running. I was smeared with blood stains but still absurdly erect. I stared at Ryman, wondering what went on behind those myopic, fishy eyes of his. I suppose there had always been Rymans in the world, men powerful enough to stage bizarre sideshows to inflame their weird, menopausal lusts. I thought of the Roman emperor Tiberius who had to torture at least one victim a day and trained young boys to pretend they were minnows and nibble at his cock as he swam naked in the Imperial baths.

His wife came back in then, still naked, and carefully washed me off with a hot soapy cloth. She angled her head so that Ryman would have a clear look at what she was doing and started blowing me. I just lay there and tried to let my body go limp. If I relaxed enough I might be able to come and end it. She'd trained her throat muscles to swallow the whole length of a penis without gagging. She took it down to the root and then glided up again, going slowly, breathing hard through her nose.

It was an incredible trick. I began to move my hips, pushing it in and out of her mouth, burying it deep in her throat. Currents of feeling began to agitate me. I felt myself grow with a sudden hardening leap until I was so big I couldn't believe she could still get it all inside her. She pumped more quickly, squeezing and retracting with the walls of her throat. Just as I felt the sperm rising to a boil, she pulled away and positioned her mouth over my inflamed penis. The hot come shot against her tongue, her lips, filled her mouth, ran from the corners down her chin. I kept coming. She licked and swallowed. Finally she sank her mouth over it and sucked me until there was nothing left.

I was completely drained. I remember getting dressed and passing a few dull, awkward words with Ryman. He looked a little peeved and tense, and was clearly impatient for me to leave. His wife just lay on the bed, spread-eagle on her back, with her lipstick and my come still smeared around her mouth. It was over and neither of them had anything to say to me. I felt like I'd opened a door and seen into a corner of their lives where nothing flourished but the obsessive, painful dream we'd just enacted. Perhaps long ago something like what we'd just done had happened to Ryman or his wife; now they were dependent on strangers to help them recreate it. It wasn't that I felt I'd done anything dirty; it was the violence, the air of repressed rage underlying everything that disturbed me. They had wanted me to play the role of a sadist who found pleasure in inflicting pain and humiliation. Where, I wondered, in a man like Ryman, did love end and hate begin?

I got an idea of it when I was standing in the motel corridor waiting for the elevator. Suddenly the silence was broken by his voice coming through the closed door. He started abusing his wife for what she'd done, accusing her of having been a whore and having enjoyed being sodomized. He vilified her for everything she'd done, describing it all in detail. It was as if he were a jealous husband who'd discovered her in the act instead of the one who'd set up and dictated the performance. This too, I supposed, was an essential ingredient, yet more emotional playacting between them. I heard a scuffling noise, the sound of a slap, a muffled female scream, and then Ryman's voice wheezing, "Now! Now, you bitch, *now!*" Then silence.

I was sure that he was then making love to her, if you can call it that.

The elderly Japanese receptionist had nodded off behind his desk. *Casablanca* was nearing its conclusion on the portable TV. Humphrey Bogart and Ingrid Bergman were arguing over the eternal subject of love: love lost, love betrayed by war and circumstance. It was easy to imagine the past as a simpler, more heroic time peopled by men like Bogart and heroines like Ingrid Bergman. But maybe it was only that Hollywood made better movies then.

I hunched my shoulders and walked quickly out of the Taj Mahal into the humid chemical light of Hollywood Boulevard. The pale, radiant night sky seemed oppressively bright, loaded with poisons generated by the city in pursuit of its pleasures. It was a light belonging to neither night nor day. Its tireless electric glare seemed to fill the boulevard with a reflection of its insomnia and its eternally restless craving. There was still traffic, the neon signs still streaked and dotted the street. I had spent less than an hour inside the motel, but it was already much later than I thought.

5

I met Leroy at noon the following day in the garden at But-
terfields' just below the Strip. He was already waiting when
I arrived, occupying a corner table shaded by a semicircle of
potted banana palms. He was dressed in a three-piece pale
green suit, an open yellow shirt and matching yellow patent-leather boots with three-inch heels. A solid gold snake
necklace circled his neck, the snake's head biting its tail in a
clasp over his throat. Leroy dug gold, jewels, platinum; he
needed a lot of trophies to feel important. A bracelet of silver coke spoons hung from his wrist; a gold stud decorated
his left ear. On the table in front of him there was a pair of
custom-designed sunglasses, a gold Dunhill lighter, an ivory
cigarette holder, and a slim Cartier pocket watch. He drove
a black Continental with white leather upholstery, the man-
datory bar in the backseat, and a telephone which didn't
work, although he always kept its aerial up to impress the
squares. In Leroy's world a man's power was reckoned by
the extravagance of his accessories. You proved how much
you had by how lavishly you squandered your money. If
pimps come up out of the ghetto on their prowess with fists,
knives, and guns, Leroy had had to rely on other qualities to

carve himself a share of the market. A black man who is also a homosexual finds himself in a twilight region outside the protection of both races. Leroy had made it on cunning, imagination, and a cool mental ruthlessness.

Frail, gawky, with a long neck and an oversize head, he was constructed like a puppet. His eyes slanted, his cheekbones stood out, the face as a whole was like an elegantly carved ebony mask. His body was no more developed than that of a slender adolescent. In repose his expression had the timeless sinister blankness of a wooden idol. When he smiled, his lips curled sardonically over his teeth, his eyes lit up with an indulgent, malicious brilliance.

"Hey, Julie." His hand languidly slapped into mine. "Looking good, brother."

I pulled out a chair and positioned it to take advantage of the sunshine. Leroy slid a plain white envelope across the bamboo table.

"Three hundred dollars just like I promised." He looked at his hands, curled them to examine his manicure. "I finally found Joey," he sighed. "He was with another guy. I really dig that boy but he will screw off on me."

"In love again, Leroy?" I opened the envelope and glanced in at the three crisp one-hundred-dollar bills.

"I'm always in love. Love is my nature. But all you pretty studs want to do is break my heart."

I stuck the money in my shirt pocket and signaled the waitress over. "Could I have a split of champagne? Moët & Chandon. You can put it on my friend's bill."

Leroy arched his eyebrows. "You made quite a hit with the Rymans." He chuckled.

"Oh yeah?"

"They want you back."

"Thanks, but no thanks."

"You don't dig the rough stuff, is that it?"

"Ryman is not my idea of fun, Leroy, and you know it."

"Do I detect a tone of bitterness in your voice, my man?"

"Forget it. I got my own clients. I don't need anyone else's action."

"That include Anne's?" he sneered.

"Yeah, more or less."

"I don't know why you fool with that bitch. I happen to know she takes fifty-fifty from you."

"Anne's got a job coming up for fifteen hundred dollars in a week. They need someone who speaks Swedish. I get to talk to the client. I don't have her husband jerking off in the same room with me. I don't have to beat up on anyone. Can you get me that?"

"Lighten up, Julie."

"I don't like being lied to."

There was a resentful silence. Leroy drummed the table top with his fingertips, his eyes flickering in short sweeps around the garden. "Watch out for Anne," he said harshly. "She'll sell you out. A little birdie tells me she's not happy with you."

"But *you* really care about me?"

"Don't knock it, man. You walk a thin line. I know you got all those rich cunts lined up. Once-a-month tricks. A little tennis, an orgasm, a dip in the pool. But if those cunts turn on you, you're through."

"I got my own scene going, Leroy. I take the jobs I want."

"Is that right?" He nodded with mock awe. "Let me tell you something, Julian. Something I learned a long time ago. There's three things I don't believe in. I don't believe in bisexuals. There is just no way anyone can be straight and bent at the same time. I don't believe in weekend junkies. A guy who shoots dope on weekends is just a tadpole about to turn into a full-time frog. And I don't believe in amateur gigolos. Now you may hang out in libraries, Julie, and move with the classy white folks and jazz them with your foreign languages but you ain't fooling anyone but yourself. No matter how groovy you are, you're still a cat who fucks for money. They may pretend to accept you but deep down that's all you are to them. You dig what I'm saying? The second it stops being convenient for them, you're out in the cold."

"I don't work like that. I've got personal relationships with my tricks."

"You and every hustler," he scoffed. "I get so tired of that same old jibe. I'm telling you none of your tricks gives a fuck. That is just the hustler's big illusion. But hustling is a reality. You go confusing the two, you going to wind up punished."

"By who?"

"I'm telling you, I'm the man. I'm your protection, Julie. I care about you more than any of your clients do."

"Knowing that's going to make me sleep a lot better." I shrugged and got to my feet.

"What about your champagne?"

"You have it, Leroy. And don't worry so much about my welfare. I don't dig being threatened."

"My man!" He lifted his hands and spread them open. "I ain't threatening you. That was just some friendly advice. You think about what I said. You got the Ryman trick anytime you want."

"Sure," I said. "I'll see you around, Leroy."

6

"Excuse me, Mr. Cole." Miss Breame, my hotel receptionist peered at me over the half-moon lenses of her bifocals. She was red-haired, in her sixties, with a pointed nose, long dry cheeks, and a prunish, critical mouth. She had never liked me very much. "I'm sorry, Mr. Cole," she said.

"Why are you sorry, Miss Breame?"

"There is someone waiting in your room. A young woman. She said she was your sister and you were expecting her."

"Really? How long has she been waiting?"

"Since early this evening. I was not aware you had a sister, but in the circumstances . . ."

"Thank you, Miss Breame." I crossed the lobby and took the stairs slowly, closely observed by Miss Breame from behind her desk. She worked the switchboard and listened in to my calls and had formed a very bad impression of my life-style from all the women who phoned me.

I stopped outside my door and listened but I couldn't hear anything. I didn't have a sister and I couldn't think of anyone who would have the nerve to pretend she was my sister in order to get into my room. I turned the handle and shoved the door open with my foot.

The French woman from the Polo Lounge was sitting cross-legged in the middle of the floor with a book open in her lap. She glanced up at me, gave me a cool examination, dropped her eyes and appeared to complete a sentence, and then closed the book with a sigh. It was done with the kind of casual, mundane air that grows up between people who've lived together for years. It wasn't the reaction I expected at all.

I didn't come into the room. I just stood in the doorway frowning at her, incensed that she was even there.

"How did you find me?" I said.

"You are not hard to find," she said. "Are you unpleasantly surprised?"

It was a very confusing, ambiguous position. I was torn by conflicting impulses, wanting to tell her to clear the hell out, but held back by that instinctive politeness you feel when someone is inside your home. This was the one place where I could be myself, and she'd violated it. I was really very rattled by her being there. It was as if my two separate identities—my private and professional ones—were suddenly being confronted with each other. It embarrassed me in a way that seemed entirely out of proportion, which makes me think she'd touched some very deeply buried fear of discovery in me.

"What do you want?" I said.

She cast her eyes around the room, taking in the sagging book cases, the El Greco and Goya prints on the walls, the stacks of sheet music piled on the baby grand piano. She was being as annoyingly high-handed as she possibly could, as if she had every right to be there and do as she pleased.

"I would have thought you lived in a place with soft

lights, thick carpets, big circular bed, mirrors on the wall—
you know, that sort of thing."

"This is where I live. Women don't come here." I came
into the room and tossed my coat on the bed. I opened the
closet and took out another jacket.

"Are you going out?"

"What does it look like?"

"Business?" she asked.

"Maybe."

"Isn't it a little late?"

"Isn't it a little late for you, *Madame Hasard?*" I widened
my eyes in a meaningful stare.

"How flattering that you've remembered my name." She
laughed disdainfully. "My husband's still in New York. I'm
alone."

"I don't care where your husband is, frankly."

"That's funny. Neither do I." She tried to hold my eyes,
but I wouldn't look at her. Her last remark hung in the air.
Her expression stiffened as she forced herself to go on.

"The other day you said fifty dollars can buy a lot. I came
to find out just how much."

"You must be mistaken," I said. "I don't do that."

"Do what?"

"What you're thinking about."

She toyed with the book, frowning sullenly, fighting to
keep up her tough front. You could see she absolutely despised herself for being in such a humiliating position. Finally she blurted out, "Why are you doing this to me?"

"Doing what?" I answered coldly.

"Humiliating me." Now her eyes were full upon me, hot
with feeling and pain. "How do you think I feel? It's not
easy for me. I've never . . . the other day you told me what
you did for a living. I came here. I found you. I want to

know what it's like." She bit her lip and got the next words out with difficulty. "I want you to fuck me. I have money. I am as beautiful as your other women."

Don't ask me why I do things. Suddenly I felt charmed by her. I could see how her resistance and pride had fought against her curiosity. She must have engaged in an incredible battle with herself to even consider doing anything so rash and impulsive as palming herself off as my sister to get into my hotel room.

"What were you reading?" I nodded at the book in her lap.

"*Le Rouge et le Noir*. You must like Stendhal. You've marked passages on almost every page."

"Yes, it's my favorite."

"Tell me," she smiled, "were you named after Julien Sorel?"

"I changed my name to Julian when I was eighteen. Julien Sorel was my hero."

"Oh, I like that." Her eyes sparkled with amusement. "That is very good. Only an American would do something so outrageous. A Frenchman would be too embarrassed to take his name from a famous novel. But now you have to tell me your real name."

I didn't answer. I closed the door and drew the drapes shut and one by one switched off the lights. Then I slipped out of my shoes, unbuckled my belt and let my trousers drop to the floor. When I was completely stripped, I padded across the floor and knelt beside her in the darkness. Her body trembled as I unbuttoned her blouse and unhooked her skirt. Her hands flowed over my arms and chest and descended down my stomach. She gripped my erection with both hands and whispered in a faint voice, "Oh God, what is your name?"

I didn't answer. When she started to speak again I covered her mouth with my lips and brought my hand down across her breasts and stomach until I was plying the hot liquid silkiness between her legs. Her underpants were soaking and warm as I peeled them off. She was so excited she came after the first half a dozen strokes.

In the night, when she cried out emotionally at her pleasure, she called me *cher Julien,* and afterwards, smoking in bed, with the room softened by flickering candlelight, she playfully referred to me as *Monsieur Sorel.*

As I was drifting off to sleep, I wondered why I'd confessed to her that Julian Cole wasn't my real name. It made me apprehensive and at the same time strangely excited. I felt like someone who tells a secret to a stranger on a train, knowing he will never see the person again. It had been so long since I'd tapped any of the real experiences that had made up my past that I hardly knew where to begin. I didn't even believe I wanted to begin. Truth was a foreign country to me, somewhere I'd lived long ago, from which I'd escaped, or exiled myself. Now approaching its frontier for the first time I felt like a traveler uneasily aware that his passport is out-of-date and he has forgotten the language of the country.

7

Michelle was still asleep when the bedside phone woke me the next morning. It was an old client of mine, Lisa Williams, calling to make a date for that evening. Suddenly, without even thinking about it, I was Julian Cole again, on the job, all the events of last night forgotten. Lisa was a phone freak; she liked to talk obscenely about what she was going to do to me. That particular morning, in order to impress on Michelle that the events of the night hadn't changed anything, I made a point of letting her see just what I did for a living.

"Oh, don't say that, Lisa," I laughed. "You're getting me aroused just thinking about it. I'm lying here getting a hard-on and it's not even ten o'clock yet."

Michelle stirred next to me. Her eyes were still closed but her breathing was shallow and I was sure she was listening.

"Oh, now you're just teasing me. Stop talking like that or I'll have to hang up and jerk off right now. . . . You like that idea, don't you? A hundred dollars? We're lying here talking about having fun and getting aroused and you're talking about a hundred dollars? How much is your husband worth? Half a million? And you're telling me you can't afford an extra hundred dollars to have more pleasure than you've had all summer? Lisa, Lisa, just listen to yourself. How can you say that?"

I glanced over at Michelle. She was observing me, lying very still, with her hands folded under her cheek. I must have already been afraid of her, already sensed her potential to affect my emotions. I know I consciously tried to repel her by what I was doing.

"Can you hold a second, Lisa? There's someone at the door." I covered the receiver with my hand and smiled at Michelle. "Good morning." I gave her a polite kiss on the nose and asked her what she would like for breakfast.

"Just you," she said.

"Coffee, orange juice, eggs, croissant?"

"That sounds delicious." She made a face.

I got back on the phone. "I'm sorry, Lisa, this is really embarrassing. There are some people here and I have to hang up. I'll pick you up at six. See you then, love."

I replaced the receiver, swung my legs out of the bed, and did an enormous stretching yawn. I rubbed my eyes and ran my fingers through my hair. After a moment I turned and looked at her.

"Well?" I said. "What do you think?"

"About what?"

"Did you make the right decision in coming here last night?"

"I'm sure I did."

"Was it what you expected?" I stood up and stretched again, yawning loudly.

"No, it was like sleeping with a real person. I'm not used to that."

I didn't really want to know what she was used to, or have her confide her problems to me. Once I started exploring her life outside the room I'd be roped into all kinds of complications.

Over breakfast she was calm and subdued, maintaining an easy, cheerful front. She had dressed while I was cooking and was obviously not intending to linger. I kept waiting for her to make a move toward me, to refer to the night we'd spent together, to reveal her possessiveness but she refrained from doing it. It was a relief that she was so cool, though it puzzled me as I'd thought she'd really been moved by our lovemaking.

I finished my second cup of coffee, placed my napkin on my plate and stood up from the table. She immediately stubbed out her cigarette and began putting her make-up in her purse.

"What do you do today?" she asked casually.

"I've got to go to the health club." That's the difference, I thought, between dealing with a client and having a woman spend the night in your place. Suddenly I was talking about *having* to do things instead of simply stating that I wanted to go to the health club. I was having to account for my time away from her, worrying whether it would injure her feelings.

"And you'll see your friend tonight?" she said.

"She's not my friend," I said casually. "She's an older woman who pays me to have sex with her."

She snapped her bag shut, smoothed her hair, and gazed at me with a grave warm expression in her eyes. "I want to apologize." She smiled.

"For what?"

"I was rude and insulting when I came here. I treated you badly in the Polo Lounge. You were very kind to me. I've had a good time with you."

"I have, too."

"So I guess I learned a lesson."

I could tell she was starting to like me too much. She could see that clinging to me wouldn't get her anywhere so she was trying a different tack: being scrupulously honest, undemanding, sweetly contrite. It was just another way of trying to get close to me.

"I was rude, too." I shrugged indifferently.

"Do you remember what you said last night?"

"Yeah."

"Do you say that to all your women?" She tried to appear amused.

"Yeah." I was hurting her, confusing her, and I could see it was only going to get worse.

"But I was different, wasn't I?" she said with a gentle, calm authority.

"What do you mean?"

"You said women didn't come to your room and then you asked me to stay overnight."

"That's true. You're different in another way, too."

"You mean I'm young?"

"No, the price." I opened the door for her. "It was awfully cheap."

She gathered her purse and coat, smiling pensively to herself, appearing not to react to what I'd said. At the door, she kissed me lightly on both cheeks, keeping her eyes averted from mine. At the last moment I expected her to suggest we get together again but she only murmured, "Thank you, darling," and walked out the door.

She couldn't have been easier or more pleasant in the way she'd handled her departure.

After she left I tried to play the piano. I'd been practicing a Scott Joplin rag for weeks, a very swift, elegantly intricate piece of music that usually cleared my mind, but that morning I couldn't concentrate on it. I told myself I'd done her a favor by treating her coldly. A married woman like her didn't need the destructive, doomed experience of an affair with a professional gigolo. Yet for some reason I wasn't satisfied with this interpretation; somewhere I had a feeling that life had presented me with an opportunity which I hadn't had the courage to explore. It annoyed me to think that she was actually a freer, more adventurous spirit than I was, with more nerve and heart than me. I was only twenty-five; those weren't qualities I was used to thinking of myself as no longer having.

8

The ocean was placid and from the height of the cliffs, appeared completely smooth; the gray-blue water was domed by an evening sky in which you could already see the first faint stars and a transparent slice of moon. On the horizon a terminal rose glow was dissolving, being eaten by a mass of dark air that seemed to rise from the vanished sun like smoke. The air was soft and windless; a sea-smell wafted up the cliffs, mingling its hint of brine with the menthol scent of the eucalyptus, the dusty odor of sage, the strong perfume of the flower-filled gardens along the street.

I left my car parked several hundred yards down the hill and climbed the rest of the way to Lisa Williams' home. I walked slowly, enjoying the evening. The street was deserted and as silent as a private cemetery. Only the Mercedes Benzes, the Cadillacs, and Rolls-Royces parked in the driveways told you that people were home.

Lisa was standing waiting in the doorway when I came up the garden path. She closed the door behind her and motioned me to get into the Jaguar angled in the driveway. She vanished back into the house and came out a moment later with her coat and hurried across the lawn. She was a tall overblown woman with an extravagantly curved figure and an incongruously plain freckled face. She had rather small, malicious green eyes, a thin deadpan mouth, and masses of curly brown hair. Her husband owned mining concessions in Rhodesia and South Africa, where they had lived before moving to Los Angeles. Lisa was snobbish, outspoken, hard-drinking, with that chilly horsiness which English women cultivate as a mannerism. She was almost hopelessly frigid. After our first few times in bed had proved unsuccessful, I asked her if there wasn't perhaps something she liked doing which she hadn't mentioned to me.

"Oh, darling, I've never *liked* it," she said. "It's just marvelous exercise."

If she had a fetish, it was talking about sex; but after a long verbal buildup, the act itself usually left her curiously flat and unmoved. What she really liked was going to public places with a young man and being seen. Once she admitted to me that the going-out part was what she really enjoyed; the sex afterwards was just something she felt she ought to do.

"But why?" I'd asked her.

"Because it's paid for and I can't stand to waste my husband's money."

That was Lisa all over. Still, I counted her among my friends. She took an interest in me, especially in anything connected with classical music. She had found me my piano and paid for a year's course of study with the music teacher who taught her daughters. I got tickets in the mail to the best concerts and plays in Los Angeles and she had made me several beautiful gifts of antique music boxes. When I told Leroy that I had personal relationships with some of my clients I was thinking of ones like Lisa Williams who had gone out of their way to further my development.

That night we had an early dinner at a small English restaurant on the Strip and then attended a viewing and auction at Sotheby Parke-Bernet, the auction house. Lisa didn't bid and hardly looked at any of the lots. Her attention centered on the crowd milling through the exhibition rooms, on the lookout for friends. It was understood that she would always introduce me as her interior decorator but this didn't fool very many people. Lisa knew it and, I suspect, secretly liked people guessing that I was, in fact, her lover.

I was hoping she wouldn't invite me in when we got back from the auction but she insisted on having a nightcap. Her husband wasn't due back until much later, her daughters were asleep in a distant wing, and it was the maid's night off. We had a brandy in the living room and then she led me upstairs to her private study. She drew the curtains and lay down on the green leather sofa and beckoned me over. She had had a great deal to drink, which, as usual, made her rather numb and unresponsive. The liquor made her want me, seemed to heat her fantasies, but her body let her down. There was a failure of connection between her thoughts about sex and what her senses could actually feel. While I made love to her, she talked, whispered, giggled, exhorted in my ear: a stream of four-letter words, childishly smutty phrases, obscene commands. Certain combinations of words would almost bring her to climax; she would repeat them faster and faster but in the end they would lose their power to excite. She would have to start on something else. No matter how I made love to her, her mind refused to relinquish control of herself; she had to dictate and manage every detail of the act.

It was never much fun making love to Lisa; something tyrannical, nervously spoiled, and eternally dissatisfied came out of her in bed. I was glad when after a number of slow buildups and failures she told me she was too sore to continue.

"It always makes me feel better," she said, "that you can't come either."

"That's very small-minded of you," I laughed.

"I know. But I used to get so annoyed with those boys Anne sent me. They would make such a production of having orgasms and then lie there all sleek and self-satisfied while I was feeling like climbing the wall. I don't think I even like men coming in me." She let out a queer, nervous laugh. "Jealousy probably. There's that one moment when they come. Suddenly they're not paying attention. They could be animals. They could be fucking anything."

I didn't think she was right but I understood what she meant. In my own way I was locked into a similar cul-de-sac by similar fears of surrendering myself. It was neurotic for, after all, the body wanted surrender, wanted a spontaneous, involuntary extinguishing of the mind. But I didn't say any of that to Lisa. I knew I gave her pleasure, at least as much as she could derive from being with a man. I made her happy, gave her confidence in her wounded sexuality which was something her husband didn't do.

At the door, she held my hand, her eyes shining, and told me she was very fond of me. "If you're ever in trouble, Julian, come to me. I mean that."

I believed her and walking down the deserted street to my car, I thought to myself how wrong Leroy was: there was a real affection between some of these women and me. There was even something like love, though the world wouldn't see it that way, feeling that the exchange of money in such a relationship wiped out the possibility of any real feeling. But people, I told myself, aren't that simple, and their feelings toward each other don't follow such hard-and-fast rules. It was a beautiful evening and I gave myself up a little to this tolerant view of my work. It meant more to me that Lisa had offered to help me than the money I'd earned, or the peacock-pride of being well dressed and sexually attractive. I felt respected as an individual for what I was, even cherished. No matter what the newspapers print about me, that was what touched me, drew me on, motivated me: that was what I was after from the world of women.

9

I was sitting by the hotel pool the next morning, glancing through the Los Angeles *Times* when I saw the headline: WIFE OF LOCAL FINANCIER SLAIN IN HOLLYWOOD MOTEL. There was too much glare in the white stucco courtyard to read easily; the sun was baking into my skin and at first I was too stupefied by the heat to take in the meaning of the words. Like a negative in an acid-bath, the newsprint seemed to waver vaguely and then it came suddenly into hard focus.

"Mrs. Arnold Ryman, aged twenty-three, wife of noted Beverly Hills financier Arnold Ryman, was found dead in a room at the Taj Mahal Motel on Hollywood Boulevard last night. The victim was severely beaten and then sexually assaulted. Mrs. Ryman was wearing valuable jewelry and carrying a large sum of cash when she went out earlier in the evening. The police suspect robbery as the motive of her assailant. No explanation for her presence in the motel has as yet been given. Her husband is helping police with their inquiries . . ."

Every muscle in my body stiffened; a cold nervous flush chilled my arms and the backs of my legs. I could see Julie Ryman with a terrible perfection of detail: the sleepy, drugged face, the smooth bronzed sweep of her hips, the red and purple bruises marbling the backs of her thighs. And her husband, with his eyes swimming in the pools of his spectacles, the clink of ice in his glass, his hoarse asthmatic breathing, the dry spit flecking the corners of his mouth. I had been in the same stale motel room with them just a few nights before; my body had pressed against hers, shared intimacies of skin and hair and penetration. My hands holding the newspaper had slapped her, my rigidly clenched teeth had bitten her breasts.

I don't know how long I sat there, feeling my blood cold and thick, and my nerves stretched with apprehension. Eventually I heard footsteps approaching and when they stopped, a shadow blocked me off from the sun. I turned and looked into the eyes of the French woman who at that moment seemed to be the last person in the world I wanted to see. She was dressed casually in a white beach dress, her hair in a green silk turban, sunglasses pushed back on her head. She looked clean and bright eyed, with a newly minted freshness about her, and something almost coltishly playful in the laughing line of her lips and the tilt of her face as she smiled down at me.

"I wish your husband would come back," I said.

"He has."

She pulled a chaise longue up beside mine and sat with one leg folded under her, lifting her face to the sun, breathing out sensually. There was a kind of cheerful confidence about her, an air of inner strength that I found very annoying at that moment.

"I can't stop thinking about you," she said.

"Try harder."

"I don't want to stop."

"Don't involve me in this," I said heatedly. "I'm not the solution to your problems at all."

"I brought money." She paled.

"I don't want money."

"Hundreds of dollars."

"Stop it."

"I can't help it," she said. "I'd give you anything. I'd give up anything for you."

"This is your fantasy. We spend one night together and you've got to make a whole emotional production out of it. You got all there was of me the other night. Don't try to drag me into your feelings." I was breathing heavily, the blood pounding in my temples, the nerves tensing around my eyes and mouth. "Who do you think you're dealing with?" I hissed. "Find a real person who's got an appetite for all this emotional need. I'm dead, baby. It's all burned out of me."

"I don't believe it," she said stubbornly. "I don't believe you're dead at all. That's just something you've been telling yourself all your life."

"What do you know about my life?"

"You're not as good at hiding as you think, Julian."

I was wild, I suppose, made reckless by images of that other young woman lying brutalized in the Taj Mahal. I suddenly grabbed Michelle's hand and pulled her up.

"Let's go," I said.

"What?"

"I don't want your money. Let's go to my room."

It was strange, very unusual sex for me that morning with Michelle. I remember sweating so heavily my eyes burned with the salt, and the sheets sticking to my wet skin, and the feel of her covered in my bathwater dampness and humidity. I was burning up with a fever, I'm sure. Even stranger was my eagerness. I was crackling with anxiety and surface tension like a nervous schoolboy. At first I couldn't even get an erection, even though I felt fiery and swollen with desire. She took me in her hand and stroked me until I was stiff and then climbed on top of me and eased me inside. She groaned with pleasure, her face slack and her eyes closed into drowsy slits. I came almost at once, and cried out, caught in surprise at the sudden sweet burning and the emotion that swelled in my throat. I lay for a long time, with her covering my body, the sweat trickling down my ribs, my hot face pressed into her neck. Everything was blank for me, a humid soft gray blankness as if I'd dozed off to sleep in a steam bath. Eventually out of that dimness I felt the muscles inside her gently working on me, squeezing and letting go like some delicate inner drumbeat. It was as if she were speaking to my sex alone, a private dialogue deeper than words, whose source had nothing to do with our personalities. The soothing, milking motion continued, and I responded and felt the rareness of it. It had an involuntary life of its own; we were like two sleepers creating and sharing the same dream, following it where it led us. Nothing like this had ever happened to me before. She had obviously mastered it; perhaps it was what she based her female faith in love on: the cornerstone of the religion she made of it, for I suspected love was like a religion to her. If allowed to, she would try to fill every crack in the world with the spirit of what could be done between a man and a woman.

But I'm getting ahead of myself; it didn't turn out so well that day. Maybe I felt I had to make up for coming so fast, or assert myself as the giver of pleasure because as soon as she'd made me hard again I took over. I began making artificial movements, lingering thrusts and circular withdrawals, touching her with my hands, rummaging through my store of techniques to bring her to orgasm. But the vulnerability and rich emotional color went out of me; I cooled and by the time she started coming I felt all the familiar aching numbness in my cock. In the end nothing was shared and I came out of her still hard, with a tight constricted feeling in the pit of my stomach.

In that mood I ended up feeling quite distant from her, even suspicious, though perhaps more from disappointment than anything else. You see, it had taken me by surprise, that sudden tide of feeling that had surged through me in our lovemaking. Surprise, because I didn't believe she really liked me but felt she was spurred on mainly by the challenge of moving someone like me. It's a kind of bravado with some women to see if they can turn on a professional. And she had something of the high priestess in her ways; she was going to demonstrate what it was all about, convert me, rescue me from my coldness. If that were so, my motives in taking her to bed that morning weren't so hot either. I'd half wanted to just humble her, half wanted something to wipe the image of Julie Ryman from my mind. So it surprised me that for these few moments we'd actually broken through into something better, though maybe it shouldn't have; people often begin affairs for the wrong reasons, as if love were such a daunting prospect they have to approach it backwards or with the appearance of doing something else.

At the time the idea of love wasn't in my thoughts and it would be false to pretend it was. Being with Michelle hadn't changed the sick dread I felt for Julie Ryman and the doomed conviction that I was somehow at fault for her death. Having mimed the very act of violence which had ended in her being beaten to death was enough to trigger every dread and guilt in my soul. I never regretted anything so much in my life.

Michelle knew something was wrong with me that day and was as aware as I was that I'd gone out of her unsatisfied.

"I want to know everything about you." She traced her finger along my lips, touched the tip of my nose, explored the hollows of my eyes. She kept her face averted a little, smiling faintly as if I was a rather amusing problem and could be humored out of my mood.

"Why?"

"Because you intrigue and fascinate me. That's why."

"We just made love, didn't we?"

"Yes."

"Then you know all there is to know," I said.

"Don't be childish. Where are you from?"

"I'm not *from* anywhere. I'm from this bed. Everything that's worth knowing about me you can learn from letting me make love to you."

"Oh, Julian. It's not important *where* you're from. It's important that you feel you can't tell me. And why should you restrict your importance to sex? You've got so much more to you. It's all those other things which make you sexually attractive. I think you actually use sex to keep your distance from women."

Of course she had me dead to rights; she'd nailed me. A client wouldn't have dared or bothered to make me confront a truth like that.

"Why do you fuck older women?" she insisted.

"What's older?"

"Forty. Fifty. Sixty."

"They pay me." I don't know why I was being so cynical. To drive her off? To keep her from seeing the despair I actually carried around inside?

"I would pay you," she said, "so would many of my friends. What's so great about older women?"

"I see younger women."

"So?"

"I prefer older women."

"Why?"

"What's the use of bringing some high schooler to climax? Some teen-ager who gets wet at the movies, who gets wet at anything? It has no meaning for me. Last week I was with a woman who hadn't had an orgasm in fifteen years. She couldn't even get any pleasure from masturbating. It took me four hours to get her off. For most of the time I didn't think I'd be able to do it at all."

"But that sounds so cold-blooded."

"She wasn't looking for romance. This woman didn't have anything. She'd gone through the best years of her life frigid. So when it was over, I had really done something. Something worthwhile. Something only I could have done. Who else would have cared enough to do it right? Young women bore me."

"Or frighten you?"

"I've already got a shrink, Michelle. You don't need to interpret my unconscious for me."

"What does he say?" She smiled.

"About what?"

"Why you're a gigolo. Why you've got this thing for older women."

"You don't really care," I said. "You're just jealous because you think it threatens you, which is foolish because you don't own me and you aren't ever going to."

"I don't want to own you. I'd like to see you own yourself."

"I don't know what you're talking about." Of course I was just hedging; I knew damn well what she was driving at.

"I bet there isn't a single person in the world you trust or tell the truth to," she said. "So how can you call yourself free?"

"Who's free? I'm not complaining about my life."

She sat up in bed and looked at me with eyes that blazed with a kind of passionate scorn. "Why do you say things like that?" she cried. "Look at the room you live in. Don't tell me you aren't interested in being something extraordinary. The only thing that really interests you *is* distinction."

"You're crazy."

"No, you're crazy," she whispered dramatically. "You have a mind, you have taste, you have talents and you hide them all under this obliging act. Do you really imagine yourself being a gigolo all your life?"

"What do you want me to do? It's what I'm good at. If there was something else, I'd do it."

"Ah, Julian." She was pained. "You don't know how fast people get used up, how quickly they lose their beauty and courage doing what you do. Why should you waste your life on all these bored women? Who made you responsible for the frigidity of the world?"

"My mother committed suicide when I was ten. My shrink says I felt responsible for her death because I'd daydreamed so much about having different parents. When she died I felt unconsciously responsible. Therefore I now sacrifice myself for older women. How does that sound?"

"Even if it's true, you could still do anything you wanted. You could become all kinds of things."

All my life I'd heard that: the doom of being promising. People always saw me in some successful role doing something where I could use my languages and social skills. I'd seriously considered studying music, becoming an expert on antiques, a professional literary translator, a United Nations interpreter, and a dozen other fields. But I'd always kept myself in reserve, saving myself for some other better destiny which was always connected in my mind with love. I didn't want to give myself up to the narrowing demands of any single profession because of that craving for some higher, greater role in life. But what a false position it had turned out to be! I knew less about love than anyone. I was in a business where it was almost guaranteed not to happen. I thought I'd been saving myself for the one great human relationship of my life and the whole time I'd been running away from the possibility of it.

Well, I didn't tell Michelle what was going on in my mind. It was starting to dawn on me that she was an extraordinary person, and maybe also a little dangerous. Dangerous to me, anyhow. An unflinching courage and pride strongly colored her personality which seemed much more dominating than mine. She was obviously a fighter for what she believed and the committed of the earth have always daunted me a little.

Anyway, our conversation ended then because the hotel receptionist telephoned up to say there was a policeman in the lobby wanting to talk to me. It hadn't particularly crossed my mind how I might be personally threatened by Julie Ryman's death. I should have been taking it into consideration. I should have been worried as hell but I wasn't. In fact, when I heard a policeman wanted to question me I was almost relieved. It would be an ordeal and in going through it, I imagined I might get some of the guilt out of my system. This was very cloudy in my mind, but I know I wanted to pay my respects somehow and face up to what had happened. I wanted to make amends, if you like, even though I was innocent which, as I've since learned, is a very suicidal attitude to present to the police.

"What is it?" Michelle asked when I put down the phone.

"Some cop bugging me about parking tickets. I've got to go down to the station to post bail before they'll accept a personal check."

The lie came out automatically, without a moment's reflection. I must have been afraid of what she would think of me for what I'd done with Julie Ryman. I guess that means by then I was starting to look at things through her eyes and caring how they appeared.

10

He was little for a cop, a delicately constructed guy with small well-made hands, and sharp regular features. He had one of those overly designed faces, the eyes bored too deep, the lips and nose too perfectly straight, that looked machine-tooled. His clothes were cheap, off the rack of a men's discount store, but they were clean and carefully pressed. Like many small men he had perfect almost bristling posture and an air of tightly constrained dignity. He was beautifully groomed, unusual for a cop, and had a deep, warm, soft voice that you would expect to find coming out of an Irish tenor.

"Julian Cole." He smiled as he came across the lobby. "I'm Detective Sunday, Hollywood Homicide. I'd like to ask some . . ."

Miss Breame's ears were wagging behind the reception desk.

"I was just going into Westwood Village," I said quickly. "Can we talk there?"

His eyes brushed over me. I was dressed in old jeans, a faded cowboy shirt, and rubber flip-flops and I don't think I was what he'd been expecting at all. He shrugged easily and inclined his head toward the door.

Outside the hotel, he turned and said, "We go over there. The coffee shop."

"It has lousy coffee."

"I like lousy coffee." His eyes hardened and he smiled by lifting his upper lip and flashing his canines. The grimace disconcerted me as did the sudden change in his mood.

In the coffee shop on Wilshire, he further confused me by ordering a glass of milk. While we waited for the waitress to bring our order, he leaned back in his chair and openly examined me. His eyes were long-lashed, dark and rich with a speculative, ironic light. Their expression was alternately playful and very hard.

Finally he frowned deeply and leaned toward me.

"I want to tell you something," he said. "I work two ways. Civilized and otherwise. I don't think you'd like otherwise."

"All right."

The waitress brought me coffee and the milk for Sunday. He tasted it with great relish. "This is *very* good," he said. "I'm crazy about milk. I don't know if I'm crazy about you yet or not. Tell me what exactly it is you do, Julian. How do you pay the rent?"

"I'm a chauffeur and a translator and I'm a part-time student at U.C.L.A. Extension."

"Studying what?"

"Art history."

"That's nice. You got a chauffeur's license?"

I started to reach for my wallet but he waved me away from it. "What were you doing last night?" he said.

"I went with a friend to dinner and then to an auction

and then we spent the evening together till about one in the morning."

"She'll verify that?"

"Of course, but I think she'd prefer to remain anonymous."

He finished his milk and thoughtfully examined the bottom of the glass. "Why anonymous?" he said.

"She's married. I gather from all this that I'm a suspect."

"You gather that, do you?" His face wore a stony expression. "This work you were doing for the Rymans—was that as a translator or a chauffeur?"

"Neither. That was more of a personal matter."

"You were friends?"

"Not exactly."

"Well, what exactly did you do at the Rymans?"

I could feel the skin of my face growing tight; my mouth was dry and bitter-tasting. "Ryman must have given you the picture," I said.

"Let's stop kidding ourselves, Julian. You fuck for money. You know it. I know it. All I have to do is book you and leak it to the press and all of Los Angeles will know it, too. Is that what you want?"

"Of course not."

"Tell me about the Rymans that night, Julian."

What could I do? I had to tell him the truth. At least most of it. It was not a story that improved with the telling.

11

Michelle had left and there was no note. She'd made the bed, emptied the ashtrays of her cigarettes, and done the few dishes in the sink, leaving no trace of herself behind. On my way back from talking to Sunday I'd been rehearsing what I'd say to back up my parking-ticket story so it was a relief that she was gone. But then I found myself faintly disturbed by the emptiness of the room. It wasn't that I missed her or wanted her there, just that I was aware of her, my mind's eye seeing her in various poses, recalling certain things she'd said. And the absence of a note bugged me, although I couldn't say why. What if I had to get in touch with her? I didn't know where she lived or what she did. Did she have children? What was her husband's profession? How old was she? It wasn't important because I wouldn't have called her if I had her telephone number, but still it bothered me all the same. She had made a pretty systematic effort to find out all kinds of things about me but I suddenly realized she had kept herself a complete mystery.

I made a stab at practicing the piano, tried reading, tried listening to my *Learn Swedish* tapes. For a while I even attempted to interest myself in watching an afternoon soap opera aimed at housewives. The day passed like that very slowly. I couldn't concentrate on anything; my mind kept filling up with shadowy flickering images of Julie Ryman.

Of course, instead of moping around like that, I should have been taking steps to protect myself. I should have been on the phone to Lisa Williams to warn her, should have consulted an attorney for advice. Why didn't I? There's no simple answer—I believe I felt that the worst had already happened and nothing I could do would change anything. And also, somewhere I wanted it to be bad, seriously bad, because something terrible really had happened and it seemed fitting that it shouldn't just pass away and be painlessly forgotten.

Everytime there's a well publicized murder the police get a few cranks eager to take credit for having committed it. There was undoubtedly a little of that craziness in me, some overly sensitive side that wanted to suffer for her death. And maybe it's not so crazy after all, for these cranks are testifying to something universal by their confessions as did the poet John Donne when he wrote, "No man is an island," since the death of one diminishes life in all others. If there was a bell tolling for Julie Ryman, it was certainly tolling hard for me that day. It was only the second time I'd had any personal experience of death, the first being my mother's suicide when I was ten. I felt very low remembering all that.

So when Alma Lautner, a client, phoned and asked if I was available that evening, I jumped at the chance of getting out. She wanted me to escort her to a political fundraising banquet at a downtown hotel and I thought that was just what I needed, something loud and distracting where you couldn't hear yourself think.

Alma Lautner was the widow of John Lewis Lautner, one

of the first great California property speculators. Almost every piece of land he ever bought turned out to be either prime real estate or rich in oil. Even his apparently useless holdings turned out to be in the way of a proposed freeway or municipal viaduct, so he had made much of his fortune from selling property to the city. He had left Alma one of the richest women in the western states. Alma had no interest in business but she wasn't averse to using her wealth to bankroll various political candidates in their election campaigns. She was at least sixty-five, an upright angular woman with the posture of a West Point cadet, and a plain severe way of dressing. She was somewhat lantern-jawed, with florid cheeks, and a powerfully hooked Bourbon nose. Her eyes were a pale scalding blue, her mouth rather misanthropically twisted down at the corners. With that kind of money and those imposing dowager looks, she scared the hell out of people. However, I'd always admired her for her outspokenness. She said just what she thought on every occasion.

"I'm no better than anyone else," she used to tell me. "I'm just so old and so rich I can afford to tell the truth. It's the only benefit wealth gives you. You don't have to scrape around flattering people. The trouble with this country is that people think being rich gives you carte blanche to act like a son of a bitch. My husband was a son of a bitch. He was born poor and died worth over forty million dollars. No honest man can do that in this country. I was born well-off. I was told that obliged me to be generous to people less fortunate than I."

Alma had an aristocratic conception of things and was one of the leading philanthropists in Los Angeles, not because she much liked people, or even had much feeling for them, but out of pride and her rigid code of honor. She was practically the only person I knew whose life wasn't dominated by a desire to make more money or become more successful.

There had never been anything physical between us; she'd made that clear from the very start. However, once, out of the blue, in the middle of a restaurant, she'd seized my face between her hands and kissed me very hard on the lips. It was done with a kind of abrupt violence, in a swooping motion, like a bird fastening on its prey, and it left me startled.

"There," she said. "It's been bothering me and now I've done it and I don't have to think about it anymore. Don't look so shocked, Julian. God made you beautiful and gave you a charming mouth. I was just paying my respects to it."

It was an eccentric thing to do, but in keeping with her character, and I truly believe she kissed me in the spirit she claimed, impersonally, as she might sniff a flower or admire loveliness in a marble statue. She never afterwards tried to repeat the intimacy.

The advantage I gained over a client by making love to her was absent with Alma. There was really nothing she wanted from me and if the mood took her she was perfectly prepared to turn that critical independent mind of hers on me.

That night, in the limousine on the way to the fund-raiser, she did just that.

"You're shining, Julian," she said.

"What?"

"Your skin, your hair. You're sparkling. You must take very good care of yourself."

"I get a lot of exercise," I said, wondering what she was aiming at.

"It must be strange for you. Wherever you go, men and

women look at you. I was born very plain and I never had that problem. I used to envy beautiful women when I was younger but I don't anymore. Beautiful people are prisoners of their looks, like you." She paused to see if I'd taken the bait, but I kept silent. "I'm fond of you, Julian," she continued, "that's why I'm telling you this. An attractive man has to be doubly strong because he affects the world violently. People respond intensely to him. Everything is made easier for him. The world tries to make him identify with his looks and take credit for them. All of this, of course, makes for a weaker individual who can be exploited. People talk about beautiful dumb blonds. What made them so dumb, if not their beauty? I'm fond of you, dear boy, but I think sometimes I'd be almost happier if you didn't have time for me. If you were my grandson, I'd say you were someone who should be doing something else with his life."

Well, that put a damper on the evening from the start and I guess I was indignant at being criticized like that. All kinds of angry answers were boiling in me and I had half a mind to let them out. Was it fair to turn around and poke holes in me for doing what in fact she paid me to do? She knew what I did for a living, what I was. I'd never claimed to be anything more. But of course, in my heart I was constantly stung by ambitions to make something more of myself. And of course she'd figured that out about me long ago and so knew where to give me the needle where it would cause maximum discomfort.

I should have been grateful for her concern. It was genuine and disinterested but it so perfectly echoed my own anxieties about my fortune I found it very unpleasant to hear. I was gloomy and my tolerance was very low for that kind of thing.

The food at the banquet turned out to be the standard

fare of lukewarm chicken, peas, and stale-looking mashed potatoes, with some pretty vile California rosé to go with it. There were about a hundred guests digging into these TV dinners, mainly couples in formal evening clothes. They were not the chic people, the show-business elite, but they represented a greater, more durable power in the state. These were the true heavyweights of California society: the city councilors, land developers, farming barons, oil-company presidents, and aerospace-industry executives. Here and there I spotted society women I knew, heiresses, widows, wives of princes of industry, the class that politicians soak for campaign contributions. It was the ultimate form of gambling for the highest stakes going in the country. You put your money on a candidate like a number on roulette and if he came up you collected your winnings after the election in the form of patronage and contracts.

A banner above the platform proclaimed: THE DEMO-CRATIC PARTY OF CALIFORNIA AND THE 22ND DISTRICT WEL-COME STATE SENATOR RICHARD STAPLES.

The name was, of course, familiar. Staples was one of the new breed of Western politicians, with film star looks, and a charismatic liberal image. He was packaged and sold as a moderate, acceptable to the left and conservative wings of the party alike. A lot of his liberalness was little more than a calculated use of cosmetics in the creation of his image. He was about forty-five, bronzed, with golden hair that had a permanent windswept look, and a jaunty grin of capped, photogenic teeth. His teeth were quite small, beady, and restless, never quite hooked up to the dazzling smile.

"Do you follow California politics?" Alma Lautner nudged me out of my reverie.

"Not much."

"You're smart. They're all whores."

I thought I was more qualified than most to discuss whores. "Look at Staples," I said. "Can you imagine the effort and mental discipline it takes to grin warmly into the faces of a hundred people? To smile insincerely at every one of them? There's a kind of greatness in it."

"You're in a very cynical mood tonight, Julian."

"No, I just recognize genius when I see it. Think of all the operators, the fixers, the slick lawyers who'd sell their mothers for an ounce more political leverage, and Staples beat out all of them for the job."

Alma chuckled but I could tell she wasn't entirely comfortable with my remarks. It was all right for her to call her candidate a whore but she didn't like it if I attacked the whole structure underlying it all. It was an attack on her too.

After dinner Staples made a short speech that was designed to have a little something for everyone in it. He wanted to help minorities and the lower income brackets without taking anything away from the class that benefited from their poverty. He said things took time. He said a lot had to be changed and quickly emphasized that it was still a great state and a great country and not to get him wrong, he'd stake his life on the free-enterprise system and a man's right to better himself. This translated as—"Don't worry out there, you aren't going to lose an iota of power or monopoly through me! No one's going to try and loosen your hold on anything."

I looked at the faces at the tables around me and wasn't overly impressed with what I saw. There wasn't a lot of benevolence in the expressions, and no great uplifting idea had brought them together. Well, they were just people and the dominant concern inflaming them was power-broking and money. They looked like those people always do—stuffed up and cut off, and watchful—with much deadness in their expressions. Someone once said that after forty a man is responsible for his face. And in many of the faces around me I saw a kind of deadness and meanness where some other human quality had been sacrificed to the overruling ambition. There were a lot of fat faces in the room, fat jowls and paunches and I knew their owners tended to consume more than they could metabolize, took more than they needed, were in danger of turning swinish.

I had seen murals of the Roman senate at the peak of its decadence and the artist had painted scenes crowded with faces and figures like these. Still, there was a certain almost criminal glamor attached to the gathering which came from the aura of power these people projected. I was by no means immune to its attractions. For all my dislike of them, I was fascinated and flattered to be present in the company of one of the most influential individuals in the room.

After the speeches Alma brought me over to the reception line to shake hands with Staples and the various party dignitaries. I wasn't paying much attention, just sticking out my hand and moving the appropriate facial muscles as the big shots streamed past. Staples himself was moving down the line toward us, his hand rising and falling, the smile working overtime. When he reached Alma his face grew especially animated and he stopped to chat with her. But I wasn't paying any attention to their conversation because I was riveted by the Senator's wife, which wasn't surprising since she'd been in bed with me that morning.

"Mrs. Lautner, this is my wife, Michelle." Staples brought her forward with a mechanical gesture, holding her shoulders as if she were a little girl being presented to an adult friend of the family. She looked straight ahead, smiled obligingly, automatically stretched out her hand to Alma. "I'm so pleased to meet you at last," she said in a hollow thin voice.

"And this," Alma said, "is Julian Cole."

Michelle looked right through me as she touched my hand. Her dark blond hair was up in a classical Empire coiffure; she had on pear-shaped diamond earrings and a gray silk evening gown. Her face was utterly composed, almost glacial in its remoteness. I tried to communicate to her with my eyes but she ignored the appeal, a tiny frown appearing on her brow. It all took less than a moment and then she was talking to the woman beside me, moving down the line, mouthing the empty greetings that went with the ritual. Staples himself gave me a keen, appraising glance and moved on without offering to shake my hand.

The incident, so swift and outwardly insignificant, wounded me deeply. I could feel my cheeks pale and my heart hammer from repressed emotion. I muttered something to Alma about having to go to the men's room and left the line.

In the mirror in the gents' room I saw myself, all the color sucked out of my cheeks, my eyes wide and nutty-looking from anger. You see, I had no experience, no training, no self-control; the first gust of jealousy I'd suffered in my life swept through me the way the common cold decimated the American Indians. I felt betrayed, tricked. Michelle's snub activated all my latent fears of social rejection. Why hadn't she told me who her husband was? I had all sorts of hard thoughts about her, that she was just as phony and manipulative as her husband. Who was she to lecture me about independence, or owning yourself, or freedom? She was a worse whore than I was, a whore on a bigger scale for that matter, since she had to lead that public life night and day. Yes, I could see now why she'd given me a false name and kept this side of her life strictly private. I was good enough to pass a morning or night with, an interesting conquest which it had amused her to make, but it ended there. Her reaction had revealed to me, I imagined, just how horrified she was to find the two sides of her life confronting each other. She had made it abundantly clear where her loyalty lay.

Well, there's no way of hiding that it shook me up and that I felt savage toward her. I was so upset it didn't even occur to me that I was behaving way out of proportion to the facts. That I already loved her was not something I could admit to myself. She'd stung me with that frozen dead-eyed glance and my only reaction was to leave at once.

When I got back to Alma she told me we'd be going on from there to a private party at the Staples' house in Beverly Hills.

"The Senator's just asked a few of us," she said. "You look frightful, Julian."

I told her the chicken à la king had made me sick and I'd just thrown up my dinner. She wasn't pleased, but there wasn't much she could do as I really was very white and unwell-looking. I begged off the rest of the evening.

On my way out I could see Michelle across the room beside the Senator, talking to a group of people. He was gripping her arm with his hand as if she were his daughter. They moved away to another group and his hand stayed clamped to her bare arm. The expression on her face had the pretty, hollow composure of a department-store mannequin, her voice when she spoke was no more than a self-effacing murmur.

And this was the woman who I'd convinced myself was extraordinary, a creature of passionate independence. This was the woman whose strength of character I'd silently admired. Colored by wounded pride, my feelings toward her had a savage sadness, for she was almost the first woman I'd ever had any illusions about.

As I moved through the guests toward the exit, a tall man with a blond moustache and a pug nose detached himself from the crowd and followed me out. I'd noticed him before, because he was one of the few people not dressed in evening clothes. I'd taken him possibly for one of the Senator's secret service guards. He went down in the elevator with me. I stopped in the lobby to pick up a newspaper and buy cigarettes and he hung around doing nothing. I went into the hotel bar, ordered a drink, and he did the same. He had a long morose face with expressionless gray eyes. His pug nose and drooping moustache gave him the mournful look of a bloodhound.

When I grabbed a cab outside the hotel, he got into a Plymouth sedan stationed right near the front door where the doorman never lets anyone park. If you were a cop you could park anywhere you wanted. This man followed me home to my hotel, drew up across the street, turned off his engine and lights and sat there. I paid off the cabbie. I was going to walk over and demand what he meant by following me but I didn't bother. It was to do with Julie Ryman's death; the police were watching me.

12

The next morning I looked for the man who'd followed me
home but I couldn't see him in front of the hotel. Perhaps
he'd been relieved by someone a little more subtle at the
job. Never having been tailed before, I found myself suddenly observing strangers in a completely new light. I took a
walk through Westwood Village, window shopping, browsing, scanning my fellow pedestrians. It was just because I
was paying so much attention that I caught sight of Michelle. She was keeping behind me on the opposite side of
the street, moving at my pace, stopping when I stopped. She
was wearing a floppy, finely woven straw hat and dark
glasses but I knew it was her. What did she want? I pretended not to have seen her, continuing to browse, but I was
no longer on the lookout for policemen. All I could think
about was her.

I went into Tower Records and shuffled through the LP
racks, keeping an eye on the door. When she didn't come in
after me I suddenly thought I might have been mistaken.
Maybe it was just coincidence that she was shopping in
Westwood that morning. I'd imagined she was following me
only because that was what I would have liked. From feel-

ing elated and excited my spirits took a nose dive. What was
the matter with me, anyway? Why should I let this woman
obsess me and make me miserable? Hadn't I decided last
night that I never wanted to see her again? I studied the
album covers, flipping through them, but I wasn't even
registering what I was looking at. I just felt worse and
worse. I couldn't bring myself to think of anything but her
and she filled me with this splitting sadness.

"Why, hello, Julian." Michelle gazed at me across the record racks, her face lit up with a not very good imitation of
surprise. "I didn't expect to . . ."

"Purest coincidence, Mrs. Staples." I made my voice light
and casual. "How are you?"

"How are you?" She looked at me carefully, trying to read
me. "Mrs. Lautner said you were ill."

"Something disagreed with me." I waved it off. "Well,
I've got to go. Nice to talk to you."

I got almost to the door before she caught up with me.
She took my arm and swiveled me around, reminding me
how she'd held on to my wrist in the Polo Lounge the first
time we'd met. Her eyes were blazing.

"What's the matter with you?"

"Me, Mrs. Staples?"

"Oh, stop calling me that."

"It's your name."

"Why do you have to be so childish?" She was quite ob-
livious of the people milling around us. "I was going to tell
you who I was. I'd have given anything for you not to find
out like that."

I was still too inwardly angry to unbend but I agreed to
talk with her over a drink. We went to a kind of pseudo-
German beer cellar, a student hangout with bare brick walls
and pewter mugs and long-stemmed clay pipes mounted on

the walls. It was fairly dark inside and almost deserted at that hour. Being with her was very painful and the idea of not being with her was just as bad. I wanted her terribly and at the same time I was so pissed off I could barely bring myself to speak to her. If this was love, I thought, they could keep it.

Right away she confessed that she'd been following me from the moment I came out of my hotel, trying to work up the nerve to approach me.

"Oh, Julian, I'm sorry I was so awful. When I saw you last night I just froze. The whole thing just paralyzed me. When I saw you leaving the reception I wanted to scream. I wanted to leave with you."

"Why did you lie to me about your name? You must have a pretty crummy idea of who I am if you think I'd make trouble for you."

"Hasard is my maiden name." Her cheeks flared with color. "I never meant to insult you."

"I've seen your husband on television. He's very impressive."

She watched me closely, trying to detect any whiff of hostile sarcasm in my remark. "I'm sure that's not your real opinion," she said sadly. "If it is, you're wrong. He's not impressive. He *is* very ambitious."

It embarrasses me to recount the course of our conversation. It's hard to believe the insistent pettiness and game-playing I put her through. I couldn't seem to stop chipping away at her, saying the opposite of what I felt to make her suffer for what I imagined she'd done to me. Maybe all lovers go through these pathetic minor hostilities, or it's simply that I have a lousy character and a crippling fear of rejection which I hide by taking the offensive.

"You just acted the way you had to act," I said. "I understand that. But you can see our worlds don't mix. We shouldn't even be seeing each other."

"Are you refusing to see me again?" she asked directly.

"What's the point, Michelle? You've got a life, a marriage. Neither of us needs this kind of relationship."

"Oh God!" She squeezed my hand. "I don't know what to do. I could never do anything to hurt Richard politically. I would die first."

"You're dying now," I said.

"Why are you saying this to me?" she cried.

"Because I know you. I know women like you. Maybe I don't want to see you throw your life away."

"I thought I loved him when we were married. I was only nineteen. I was straight out of a convent school in France. Now he wants me to have a child. Politically it looks better, I suppose." She was waiting for me to say something, pleading with her eyes. "Is it fair for me to leave him?" she asked. "To destroy his career because I made a mistake?"

"I'm a man," I said. "That is just a guilt-trip men will always try and lay on their wives. He's getting what he wants. You have to do the same. Take the pleasure when you can."

She looked at me oddly, a little rebuffed, rather hopeless for a moment. Did she want me to tell her to leave her husband because I would take her?

"And you, Julian? Where do you come in? Where do you get pleasure?"

"What are we sitting in this place talking for when we could be in bed?" I touched her face across the table. "Come home with me."

"I can't, darling. I have a lunch engagement."

"Break it."

"It's the Mayor. Richard wants me to be there." She

sighed heavily and pressed my hands. "Please, tomorrow when I've had time to think. I can't just . . ."

"Okay, think." I shrugged. "I don't know what I want from you anymore, either. Last night I was so mad at you I was sick. One minute I want to hurt you and the next minute I think I'm going to die if I can't have you." Over Michelle's shoulder I saw the door open and a man enter, descending the steps into the cellar, straining his eyes to see through the gloom and cigarette smoke. It was the man who'd followed me home from the hotel.

There was no pressing reason to try and elude him; as a murder suspect it made sense for the police to keep me under surveillance. But it still alarmed me that I was being treated like a criminal and having my activities reported on. I told Michelle I had to go and baffled her by instantly rising from the table and rushing out the back into the kitchen. There was a fire door which gave on to an alley. I went out that and ran two blocks and circled back to my hotel.

The whole exercise turned out to be a remarkable waste of time and energy because there was Detective Sunday waiting in his car in front of my hotel. He rolled down his window and called me over.

"Get in the back," he growled.

I had just got in and was in the act of shutting the door when he floored the accelerator and peeled off from the curb. My head snapped back against the seat with a painful twist of the neck muscles. I was even more alarmed by what he did next. The siren and red light came on and his speed increased with a sickening rush until we were roaring along Wilshire Boulevard at something like ninety miles an hour.

Pedestrians, oncoming traffic, and red lights didn't exist for Sunday. I braced myself in the backseat, watching the cars coming at us like a roller coaster looming out of a

Cinerama screen. He was hunched over the wheel, jerking it with quick tight movements, running in and out of the wrong lane like a man shooting the rapids. Up ahead traffic was pulling to the side of the road in front of an intersection. The lights were against us but Sunday never even slowed down, barreling across it at full speed and narrowly missing an electrician's van which braked so hard it went into a sideways spin.

"What are you doing?" I screamed.

"You lied," he shouted over the wailing siren. "We checked out your alibi. Lisa Williams says you dropped her off at ten that night. The Ryman murder was an hour and a half later. I'm taking you in, Cole."

"I was with Lisa until nearly one in the morning," I yelled. "I described her house to you, her study. I'll tell you the color of her goddamn underpants that night."

"You shouldn't have lied."

"I didn't."

"You did!"

We could have been five-year-olds having that kind of shouting match, only he was going ninety miles an hour, and if I survived the ride I was going to jail.

Suddenly he screamed to a halt just beyond the intersection of Wilshire and Santa Monica Boulevard and pulled the car into a bus stop. The siren stopped. He killed the engine. "She admitted you'd been there on several previous occasions," he said wearily, as if nothing had happened. "She said you were a musician and she was trying to help you."

"Well, what do you expect her to say? That I've been balling her for the last two years?" I was still shouting although with the siren off it was no longer necessary.

"Okay, she's got a reputation to protect. *Maybe.*"

"She is *lying*, man!" I cried. "Listen, she's got scars under her breasts where they were lifted, scars behind the ears. She's got a mole on her ass the size of a dime. I'll describe her whole body to you."

"Yeah, well I don't think it's going to sound too hot in court when you get up and start telling the jury all about the inside of Mrs. Williams' twat. Anyway, it doesn't mean you were screwing her that night."

"She lied about the one thing. She's lying about the other."

He had turned in his seat so that his head was visible to me in profile but so far he hadn't looked at me. Now he did so, with a curious, pleasant expression in his eyes. To look at him you would have thought he was in a good mood.

"How do you like my driving, kid?"

"I love it, Sunday. What do you think?"

He shook his head, grinning to himself. "You should have seen your face in the rearview mirror. You looked like you were trying to pass a kidney stone. You really been throwing it to that Williams broad, huh?"

"Sure," I said.

"And the Senator's old lady? And the woman from Charlottesville, and Mrs. Ryman, and all those others? . . . Jesus, what's your secret?"

"I eat Wheaties."

"Is that right? You take vitamin shots? Dope? How d'you do it?"

"I'm just horny all the time and I dig women and they dig me. I'll tell you, though, you keep spying on me and messing with my clients, I'm out of business. You don't want to fuck these old broads so what's it to you?"

"I'd fuck the Senator's wife," he said. "I'd lay that any day anywhere. That is what I call . . ."

"Just keep her out of it, Sunday."

"Now isn't that touching?" he sneered. "You aren't such a cool number after all. Real feelings surge under that glossy exterior."

"I'm a hustler. That doesn't make me a Martian. The Senator's wife has got nothing to do with any of this."

He took out a pack of cigarettes, shook one into his hand and rolled it around in his fingers. His eyes moved in slow, sweeping arcs, clocking the street, watching the activity. Shoppers and businessmen were passing to and fro on the pavements. We were just inside the Beverly Hills city limits. Outside the car was freedom; at least the southern California variety of it. The cheapest sunshine on the market, shops filled with everything that money could buy, French restaurants, Rolls-Royce showrooms, smartly dressed women in gleaming convertibles. It was my world but from the back of a police car it looked like something I'd never properly seen before.

"What are you grossing a month, Cole?" The policeman turned to stare at me. "For curiosity's sake."

"Whatever it is, the payments on my car and piano eat it up. I live pretty high when I'm with a client. By myself I don't care. I live in one room in an inexpensive hotel."

"How come you don't marry one of your rich clients and retire?"

"That's not what I want."

"I worked Vice in Hollywood nine years. The sewer watch. I've seen it all, Cole, but I can't figure you out. What the hell is your angle?"

"I'm not planning on doing this for the rest of my life," I said uncomfortably; suddenly it seemed like everyone was asking me the same questions, zeroing in on my weakest point. "Anyway, you didn't take me for a ride to discuss my life-style."

"Would you be willing to come in for a lineup?" he said.

"I suppose so. Sure."

"Doesn't it ever bother you?" He finally lit his cigarette and dragged deeply, letting the smoke lie in his lungs. "Don't you ever get disgusted?"

"I give women pleasure, Sunday. There are worse jobs."

"Why didn't you tell me you beat up Julie Ryman?" He slipped the question in with no change of expression.

"I didn't."

"Yeah, you said that. That's why I went back and checked it twice with the coroner. Julie Ryman's neck and arms were bruised. Older bruises. The coroner estimates she got them the night you were with her. Her legs and buttocks were also badly scratched, also made the night you were with her."

"Maybe her husband did it." It sounded lame even as I said it. Sunday had a technique of mixing hard and soft questions, of switching moods, which made even my honest responses sound unconvincing.

He took a black and white five-by-seven-inch photograph from the glove compartment and studied it. Then he handed it to me with a strange crooked smile on his face. I could feel the full watchful weight of his eyes on me.

The photograph was a do-it-yourself vomit kit on the order of pictures of war-crime atrocities. Julie Ryman's face was unrecognizably mutilated: brains mixed with blood, skin ploughed open to the bone. The blood lay in scattered spots all over her naked body as if she'd been sprayed with paint, and darkened the carpet around her head. She was lying on her stomach, her hands bound behind her back, her legs bent at the knee and spread wide apart. The picture was taken in that bright police photographer's light that seems to suck all softness and shadow out of the print. My stomach took a sudden gliding lurch and the cold sweat pebbled my face in lumps.

"She was beaten in the face with something blunt and hard," Sunday said softly. "She was bitten all over her breasts. Not love bites but what you'd expect from wharf rats. Then she was violated with the murder weapon. Maybe sometimes the pleasure you give to women gets out of hand. . . ."

I rolled down the window and tried to gulp air into my lungs, fighting to keep the contents of my stomach down. It was a hot, dry sunny day and the air was awash with chemical fumes; there didn't seem to be any oxygen in it. I remember laying my cheek against the burning chrome windowsill of the police car and gazing out like a poisoned animal at the buildings and traffic.

Sunday drove me back to my hotel in silence, no longer in any rush. Apparently he wasn't going to take me in.

When he pulled in to the curb I got out and dropped the photograph just inside his window.

"I don't want it," I said.

"No," he shrugged. "I guess you don't need it."

"What is that supposed to mean?"

He turned the steering wheel and glided away without answering or looking at me, leaving me alone on the street with my insides twisted into a knot of horror and loathing at what I'd seen.

13

"I'm sorry, Mr. Cole." Miss Breame, the receptionist, looked at me with frightened, strangely bulging eyes. "I couldn't stop them. They had a search warrant for your room."

"What are you talking about?"

"The police. They came while you were out."

So that was it: the outing in Sunday's car had been a ruse to get me away from the hotel so they could go through my room.

"It's a misunderstanding, Miss Breame, which is going to get cleared up today. Don't you worry about it."

"I'm sure I don't worry." She shook her shoulders and head imperceptibly as if she'd felt an icy draft. "Mr. Wibak is the manager. It's for him to worry."

Miss Breame had never liked me but up to now her dislike had always taken the form of a rather frigid, pompous disapproval. The way she looked at me now you would have thought my hands were dripping with the blood of my latest victim.

"There was also a young man looking for you before the police came," she blinked.

"What did he want?"

"He wouldn't say. He seemed to know where your room was. I told him he couldn't go up and he went away."

"What kind of young man?"

"I'm sure I don't know," she snapped. "He was blond and quite short and he didn't want to leave a message."

I thanked her for the information and took the stairs two at a time up to my room. I'd lived in the hotel for nearly two years, but if the police kept up their harassment, the management was bound to insist I leave. They were not too hot on me anyway because of my piano and the odd hours I kept.

My room reeked of cigar smoke and looked like the scene of a burglary. The bed had been disassembled, the carpet rolled back, the shelves cleared of records and books, the dresser drawers emptied on the floor, the lining paper ripped out. The ventilating ducts had been removed, the fridge emptied out, the toilet cistern drained. My curtains were down, the back of the TV screwed off. There were dirty fingermarks around the skirting board and moulding where they'd felt for loose sections. Inside the open piano there was a feathery whorl of cigar ash lying on the cables and a burn mark on the lacquered top where one of them had laid a lit cigar.

But the thing that crushed me most was that they'd taken my diaries. The idea of Sunday reading descriptions of my most private thoughts and fears, my sexual problems, my painstaking efforts to overcome my obscure background, filled me with a kind of shameful panic.

In retrospect the confiscation of my private diaries was a turning point in my relations with the police. From that moment on I considered them as being maliciously and actively against me. It was a waste of time to expect either help or fair treatment from them. Someone was trying to frame me and it looked like the police were going along with it. How could Lisa Williams have lied, knowing what it meant to me? From the moment I lost my alibi, events speeded up and ominously darkened; everything I did became tinged with desperation.

14

I didn't bother to phone Anne Laughton to warn her I was coming. I didn't even make any attempts to shake the police tail that followed me to her office. Her receptionist was out to lunch. I pressed the bell on her desk in the anteroom which opened the connecting door to Anne's office and walked in unannounced.

She was seated at her desk in the act of pouring a shot glass of brandy from the silver flask she kept in her drawer.

"What do you want?" she said with her customary charm.

I sank down into the steel-and-leather armchair in front of her desk. It was a mistake. It was one of those chairs that tilts you back, keeps your feet almost off the ground, renders you at a disadvantage. Either you recline all the way back and feel like a patient on a psychiatrist's couch or you sit on the very edge and look correspondingly anxious and ill at ease.

Anne peered down at me, her chin cupped in her hands, smiling with an arch, poisonous sweetness. She was dressed in a frilly white lace smock, drawn tight around the neck, with yards of tentlike folds concealing the contours of her body. It looked like a Victorian nightie for a giant baby.

There were white silk ribbons in her hair, several to each of her thick blond pigtails. Her cheeks were loaded with flaming rouge and she'd painted an absurdly sinister beauty spot over her upper lip.

"Something's happened, Anne."

"I have only two words to say about that: *so what?*"

She opened the inlaid Moroccan box on her desk, took out a Kool and rolled it around in her fat fingers. She was always caustic, defensive, hostile, but that was her act. Underneath I'd always assumed she had a sneaking affection for me. It occurred to me suddenly how wrong I might be.

"Don't waste my time, Julian. You don't call. You blow in here like you own the place. What is it?"

"I think I'm in a frame."

"Who's putting you in?"

I struggled out of the chair and went to stand by the window behind her desk. Down on the street I could see the blond pug-nosed cop standing by his car with his hands in his pockets.

"It's about this Ryman murder," I said.

"You tricked with them?" I heard her swallowing her shot of brandy, then the sound of the glass being brought down hard on the desk top.

"Only once as a favor to Leroy."

"You two-timing bastard." She said it with no emotion.

"For God's sake." I wheeled around. "We're talking about a murder rap. I did one trick for someone else, that's all."

"Why don't you ask your pal, Leroy? He owes you a favor."

"Do you have to take this like a jealous wife?" I asked. "Do you think I deserve to go to jail over one lousy trick?"

She fussily straightened things on her desk and then took hold of one of her plaited pigtails and slapped it into her open palm rhythmically. It was done with the brisk, authoritarian flair of a general tapping a riding crop against his leg.

"You trick for other people. You cheat me out of money. Then when you need a favor you come back to me."

"Anne, Lisa Williams was with me the night Julie Ryman was killed. She denied the whole thing to the cops."

"Lisa Williams?" Anne's face was blank. "I used to have a client called Lisa Williams. But then someone else took her over. I have no interest in Lisa Williams anymore. As far as this company is concerned Lisa Williams no longer exists."

"You're cutting off your nose to spite your face."

Anne opened her desk drawer and removed a slim silver flask and a shot glass and poured it full of brandy. She shoved the glass across the desk to me and drank straight from the flask.

"If I help you," she wiped her lips, "you'll have to help me."

"How?"

"You'll have to come back into line. Work strictly for me. No outside tricking."

"That doesn't have anything to do with this."

"Like shit it doesn't. When I found you, you were just a skinny dropout who looked set for a career parking cars. I taught you how to treat women. Where to take them. How to dress. I introduced you to the richest women in this town. Then one day you come to me and say, 'I'm too good for you' and cut me out. Well, you're a fool. I know this business. I know what rich people are. But you're vain, Julian. You like to pretend that money is secondary because you have phony ideas about yourself. This is a business. It's not some Horatio Alger story."

"It's different now," I said. "Don't you think people change? When I'm good now, I don't even have to make love to a woman. I'm her confidant, her equal. I'm getting older. I've got to move forward."

"Where does your moving forward leave me?" She poured out another measure of brandy, capped the flask, and returned it to the drawer. "What about this Swedish woman coming in the day after tomorrow? She's wired to a lot of auto money—Saab, Volvo. I can't have you screwing up with that kind of client."

"Who's screwing up?" I protested. "I've been practicing my Swedish for weeks."

"If you let me down on this one, you're finished."

"When did I ever let you down?" I said angrily. "You've made a fortune out of me. I've brought you nothing but business from the day I arrived."

"I wouldn't go on about it." She tossed off her drink and blinked her eyes. "But I will try and do something about Lisa Williams for you. I've actually got more dirt on her husband than her. I'll ask around who else the Rymans tricked with."

"Thank you."

At the door, as I was about to go out, she smiled speculatively at me, with contempt in her eyes.

"You did it, didn't you?" she said.

"What?"

"The Ryman killing."

I couldn't believe her. She'd known me for two years and could say that to me as coolly as if she were discussing the weather.

"Is that what you think, Anne?"

"Don't worry, Julie. Nothing anyone does ever surprises me—especially in this business."

"I didn't kill Julie Ryman."

"Sure." She shrugged her huge rounded shoulders, already returning to the work on her desk. "I'll take your word for it."

Maybe it was dishonest of me to have always tried to look on being a gigolo in a positive light, ignoring the unlovely, callous aspects, and making a lot of the good I sometimes did for women. There were sides to the business and people like Anne and Leroy I'd chosen not to examine too closely. Still, that interview with Anne shook me in my foundations. It wasn't that she believed I'd done it which shocked me; it was that it didn't matter to her particularly one way or the other. In her eyes it was a question of indifference whether I was guilty or innocent. And that was my world, the kind of moral wasteland I lived in, which I hadn't seen until then, or wanted to see. It's no good pretending I was some innocent young guy who suddenly woke up one day and realized he was dealing with a lot of vicious criminal types. But on the other hand, it was a revelation to learn that the people around me didn't care if I was a homicidal psychopath or not.

I lost my police tail by driving into the underground garage of an office building on Hollywood and taking the exit ramp onto a side street before he had time to see which way I'd gone. From there I drove directly to Pacific Palisades.

A fire-engine red Facel Vega was parked in the driveway next to Lisa Williams' Jaguar. It was a weekday and I'd expected Lisa's husband to be at work but I decided to go through with it just the same. As I stood on the front porch and rang the bell, I thought of what Lisa had said to me the last time I'd stood there. Hadn't she been sincere? Surely, once she realized how important it was to me, she'd reverse her testimony to the police.

The plump Mexican maid answered the door and looked at me with round liquid eyes that seemed to widen with surprise and then go subtly flat. I'd always been on good terms with her. Her coolness now seemed like a tiny harbinger of disaster.

"*Como está*, Carlotta?" I smiled at her.

"*Señor* Cole?" Her attitude stiffened as she blocked the entrance. Behind her I could hear voices and the sound of one of Lisa's daughters practicing scales on the piano.

"Who is it, Carlotta?" Lisa's heels could be heard clacking across the wooden entrance hall. The maid disappeared and a second later Lisa stuck her face out of the half-open door. Without makeup she looked washed-out, older, rather grimly strained around the eyes and mouth. Her best feature, her eyes, which normally had a malicious, lively sparkle looked as hard and flat as nail heads.

"Hello, Julian," she said defensively. "Why are you here?"

"I have to talk to you, Lisa."

"What do you want?"

"I'd just like to clear up . . ." I took a step forward but she instantly brought the door closer to its frame. "Lisa, why did you tell the police that. It's put me in a terrible . . ."

"Yes," she cried in a weak, ringing voice. "There was a detective here. I was very surprised you used my name. We . . . we've tried to help you, tried to encourage your music. One had no idea you were leading a double life."

"What are you talking about?"

"I told the detective the truth. I cannot and will not lie to protect you."

"I was here. I was here with you until nearly one o'clock."

"I have no intention of getting involved in your sordid little affairs."

The door swung open and a middle-aged man with pale, thinning hair and a round, florid, pugnacious face stood next to Lisa. He was dressed in tennis clothes. He had oversized biceps and trunklike thighs which seemed out of proportion to the size of his head. He was blinking rapidly, his lower lip thrust out.

"What is it, dear?" he said frostily. "Is there something wrong?" His eyes darted over my person but avoided my gaze.

"This is Julian Cole. The boy who told the police I was with him the night of the murder."

Williams pulled his shoulders back and lifted his chin, looking down at me. "I've heard about you, Cole. It's bad enough my wife gets taken in by opportunists like you. But when they go spreading dirty stories about her to the police, I put my foot down. Now I suggest you get out of here."

"They're not lies."

"Get inside, dear." He put out his hand and pressed Lisa back into the house.

"I swear to God I was here."

"I know you're lying," he growled.

"How?"

For the first time he met my gaze and held it.

"Because I was here with my wife from ten o'clock that night." His face was very ugly to look at, made ugly perhaps by the lie he was telling. I don't know what it was but suddenly I lost my physical fear of him. It was he who was afraid. Almost every other Friday for the last eighteen months his wife had gone out with me, been made love to by me. Where had he been on those Friday nights? What kind of dirt did Anne Laughton have on him?

"I know karate," he said with waning conviction.

Sure, I thought, as I walked back to my car, Williams was on Anne Laughton's books, too, as interested in good-looking young men as his wife.

When I reached the end of the driveway, he shouted, for Lisa's benefit: "Go on, before I teach you a lesson."

I thought to myself—this man is lying to protect a brittle social reputation which is more important to him than whether an innocent person is sent to prison for murder.

"Why, you rotten bastard," I said, turning around and starting back toward him. But of course he scuttled back into the house and slammed the door shut. It was his door, his house, his property I was standing on. Apparently it was his world, too, because there was nothing I could do about it. Leroy had been right: the instant I stopped being convenient to Lisa she'd dropped me. The timing was deadly: it was just when I was over an abyss that she'd chosen to do it.

15

Wibak, the hotel manager, waylaid me in the lobby when I got back. He was a Polish immigrant, a slightly built guy in his late twenties with wild curly hair and bulging radiant brown eyes. He didn't have a lot of chin, his teeth protruded, there was something wet and dazed about his smile, but the overall impression was pleasant. He wasn't the stuff that hotel managers are usually made of at all. He was very nervous and in awe of everyone including the staff he was meant to manage. They all took advantage of him because his English was bad. Wibak had played the oboe in the National Polish Youth Orchestra in his teens and was still an accomplished musician. He dreamed of one day finding time to practice again and of perhaps gaining a place in an American orchestra. He sometimes invited me to listen to music in his room. It was Wibak who'd fought for me to be allowed to have the baby grand piano in my room.

"Mr. Cole, come." He led me nervously to the end of the lobby out of Miss Breame's earshot. "You know we very much like you. Much good friend of the hotel always, Mr. Cole."

"Sure."

"This is terrible business with police. Miss Breame has big mouth, tell all the people in hotel."

"I was furious," I said with great concern. "Furious. It's been a terrible mistake."

"Mistake. Yes?" He looked at me hopefully.

"They were looking for a Julian Coleman. Wrong name. Wrong person. I made a big protest, Wibak, and told them we were prepared to sue."

"No sue," Wibak said. "Not necessary to sue."

"But the police will send an official letter of apology and pay for any damages to the room."

"Ah, good news!" He clapped his hands. "Now Miss Breame shut the mouth of gossiping. Now all is understood."

I felt lousy feeding Wibak a line of goods like that but I needed time to think. As I crossed the lobby, Miss Breame rapped a key on her countertop to attract my attention. Her eyes were frozen over with disapproval.

"Your *sister* is waiting in your room," she said. "She insisted I let her in."

"Fine."

"She called down to the desk and thought your room had been robbed. I'm afraid I was forced to tell her the room had been searched by law-enforcement officers."

"That's very thoughtful of you, Miss Breame. Please tell as many people as possible. I'd like the news to get around."

The door to my room opened before I could turn the key in the lock. "Julian, I thought you'd never come." Michelle flooded into my arms, pulling me inside. "I've been so worried . . ."

"You shouldn't come here." I disengaged her hands from around my neck. "It isn't safe anymore."

"Stop it." She embraced me again. "I want to be with

you. Do you think my feelings have changed because you're in trouble? I don't care what you've done."

"You can't say that until you know."

"My father was in the Resistance." She held my head between her hands. "Also my uncles. All died in the hands of the SS. Even my mother was arrested and tortured. She was not afraid. I am not afraid either. If I have your love I am not afraid of anything." A crisis brought out her passionate nature: she was one of those stormy, proud characters who almost welcomes a disaster for the opportunity it gives her to prove her love. It wasn't that I doubted her sincerity, but I felt afraid for her. She was just the kind of rash, romantic woman who'd wreck her life out of an impulse to sacrifice herself.

"I don't expect you to be frightened," I said. "But you might be horrified. I'm no hero of the French Resistance like your father, Michelle. I'm a goddamn Beverly Hills gigolo."

"What does that matter? I see beyond that."

"You mean you see me giving it up."

"Is that so shocking?"

I took her by the hand and led her to the couch. "Yes," I said. "I'm afraid it is. What else do you see me doing? None of the things I like would provide me with a living. No one's going to pay me to study music, or sit on my ass in a library reading books. Why should they?"

"I have money, Julian. You would have all the time in the world to find an agreeable career for yourself. You could go back to the university."

"I've had time," I said. "Look what I've done with it. It's too late to kid myself anymore. I didn't have to be a gigolo and you know it." I was arguing passionately for something I didn't even want to believe in: my unsuitability for any normal role in life. "Anyway," I added, "I wouldn't let you support me. I'd rather wash cars."

"You mean all those old women can support you," she retorted hotly, "and I can't give you anything?"

"If I quit I'm totally vulnerable. I become completely dependent on you."

"Then we'd be even," she said. "I'm already in that position."

I knew she was right; she'd put herself on a limb for my benefit. It just terrified me that I wouldn't have the stamina to support a long-term emotional relationship, or even the chance to try.

"I'll tell you why the police searched my room," I said. "They think I killed the Ryman woman, the one in the papers. Two nights before she died I was with her."

"But you were with me the night she was killed."

"No, I was with another client. The woman who phoned that morning we were in bed together. She's denied the whole thing. Her husband is backing up her story."

"But it's your word against theirs," she protested.

"The word of a gigolo isn't worth much, Michelle. Someone somewhere out there is setting me up for this thing. I don't know who and I don't know why. For all I know this room is bugged and the phone is tapped. The cops even know about you."

"Let them know!" she cried. "We're in this together."

Her loyalty was so spontaneously given, I felt overwhelmed by it. I pulled her into my arms and kissed her face, her hair, her neck. She was wearing an ankle-length Indian robe of pale blue silk tailored to hug tightly to the contours of her body. A dozen carved buttons ran from the waist to the throat. I started to undo them but it took too long. I caressed her breasts through the smooth fragile material instead and felt her nipples harden with desire. She stayed perfectly still, watching me, with a calm kindly light in her eyes. I didn't understand why she wasn't responding. She was usually actively reciprocal in our lovemaking. Looking at her, sitting with her legs crossed under her, with fine upright posture, her shoulders square, her face inclined slightly, I felt a surge of tenderness for her. She was so finely made, with such a melting lovely expression on her face— her value suddenly came home to me. I eased her backwards on the couch, kissing her gently at first and then with increasing passion as my hands explored her breasts and thighs. We caressed each other like that through our clothes for several moments until I started to draw the silk gown up her thighs.

"No, not yet." She held my wrists.

"Huh?"

"Please, Julian. I don't want to fuck yet."

"Why not?"

"Let's just be like this some more."

So we returned to caressing and kissing each other but I was baffled by her reaction. I was hard and she could feel me against her. When my hand caressed between her thighs I could feel how hot and wet she was through the material. Her breathing was progressively deepening, but again, when I tried to roll her gown up her hips she locked her hands around my wrists.

"What's wrong?"

"I just want to make out some more." She kissed me.

I pushed her back, baffled.

"Michelle, you love to make love. What's wrong?"

"I love to be with you, to talk to you. I love it when you kiss me, when you touch me . . . but not when you fuck me. Because when you fuck me you go to work."

She pressed her face flat against a sofa cushion and sighed.

"But you loved to make love before."

"That was before."

"Before what?"

"Before I cared about you."

I moved over her and began touching her again but she didn't respond.

"You're supposed to understand women, Julian," she said. "Why can't you see how frustrating it is for me not to be able to give you any pleasure? I'm not blind. I see the way you dramatize your orgasm just to give me pleasure. Such a big production, but you really hold yourself above everything. Always at a distance. Always in control."

"But I love to give you pleasure."

"You tell others to take pleasure but you won't take any for yourself. You won't let yourself go."

"But I get pleasure from pleasing others."

She sat up and smoothed her hair and then stroked my cheek. "It's funny," she said. "My whole married life I've been like you, trying to please my husband, sacrificing my wishes for him. It gave me the upper hand and I had a good conscience. I was brought up to think of pleasing others first. But over the last year my conscience hasn't been so good. I began to realize that I wasn't really unselfish, but only afraid. . . . I didn't have the courage to take what I wanted. I'd made a virtue out of my weakness, that's all. I want you to have the courage to take what you want from me. Does that sound so strange?"

"It scares me," I admitted. "I don't know if I can do it."

"It scares me, too, darling," she smiled, "but I wouldn't love you without your fear."

At that moment it seemed an extraordinary thing she was

saying. She had seen through my defenses to a buried person who I'd never dared let out. Always before in my experience the world had been content to take me at face value and question no further. Now suddenly here was a woman rejecting what all the others had accepted, and demanding for herself what I'd always thought of as the private, inwardly damaged part of my being.

We did everything we could think of to each other except fuck that evening. We were like two teen-agers on a couch, circumventing the fact we had no contraceptives. It was innocent, perverse, outlandish, childish eroticism which I'd known as a young adolescent and forgotten still existed. She made me come in her hand and then later put me between her breasts and made a soft warm tunnel of them, finally taking me into her mouth when I started to come. They say that men and women fall in love easily in wartime. Neither of us knew that night what would happen the next day, or if we would ever be allowed to see each other again. There was something urgent and pure, some added dimension that gave our glances and caresses a special radiance and meaning that night. When we finally made love it was done with a kind of endlessly gentle mutual submission, as if we were trying to conceive a child and wanted it to be the fruit of everything that was most passionately tender between us.

16

It was an interlude only, for the nightmare reasserted itself almost instantly the next morning in the form of the blond pug-nosed policeman. He was leaning against his car across the street when we came out, with a look of deadly boredom stamped on his face. I walked Michelle to her car and then returned to the hotel entrance and paused. I had noticed a man standing by the entrance when we came out. He was a young man with red hair slicked down and carefully parted, dressed in a light tan Ivy League suit and silk striped tie. He wore horn-rimmed glasses; his face was chubby, and rather immature. He looked like a young lawyer, or stockbroker. He had been leaning against the side of the building reading *The Wall Street Journal* and now I noticed he had moved about ten yards down and was leaning against a car, watching me over the top of his newspaper. When I caught his eye he looked down and made a production of being deeply preoccupied with what he was reading.

The police were watching me but they made no pretense of the fact. Who was this character who looked like a chubby, pompous, prep school boy?

I carried on to the corner and joined a group of people

lined up at a bus stop. There was a long wait, and by the time the bus came about ten people had joined the line behind me. One of them was the policeman. Several places behind him was the man in the horn-rimmed glasses. At the last minute I stepped out of line and hurried off toward Westwood Boulevard.

The policeman plodded after me, keeping about a half a block between us, slouching along with his hands in his pockets. The man in the horn-rimmed glasses was quite another matter. Every time I turned around he was doing something flamboyantly ordinary and matter-of-fact—lighting his pipe, tying his shoelace, folding his newspaper, examining a shop window, checking a street number.

I had stopped in front of a shoe store and could see him reflected in its window. He was studying the menu of a Hungarian restaurant across the street. The restaurant had been closed for repairs. I turned and ran across the traffic and came up behind him without him seeing me.

I touched him lightly on the shoulder.

"I couldn't help noticing you were following me," I said in a soft velvety voice. "I'd love to buy you a drink."

He jumped back, flushing to the roots of his hair, gripping his newspaper to his chest. "I'm sorry," he blustered. "I don't know what you're talking about."

"Don't be shy." I came closer. "I think you're terribly attractive."

"Excuse me." He started to walk away. "You've made a mistake. I'm not . . ."

"Don't be silly." I kept pace with him. "I love meeting new people. Most people are so uptight they're afraid to just talk to each other. My name's Julian. I'm a Scorpio. Cancer rising. That's why I'm moody. It's my rising sign. I'll bet you're a Taurus. You're so determined-looking."

"Leave me alone," he muttered, staring straight ahead, lengthening his stride.

"Leave *you* alone?" I caught him by the shoulder and swiveled him around. He knocked my hand loose, his eyes widening in alarm. "I couldn't do that," I said in a soft, menacing voice. "I'm not going to do that. I'm going to break your glasses and make you cry. That's right, I'm going to beat the shit out of you. . . ."

He backed away from me, looking up and down the nearly deserted pavement for support. I don't know where my nerve was coming from. Although flabby, he was bigger than me, and I didn't know the first thing about fighting. I suppose, if worse came to worst, and he started to beat me up, I was counting on the policeman to intervene.

"Who's paying you?" I advanced on him with my fist cocked.

"What are you talking about?" He backed up, stumbled against the steps of an office entrance and came to rest against a plate-glass door.

"I'm going to put you through that glass door face first," I muttered. From watching movies and television, every American knows the nominal etiquette of violent confrontations, and I was no exception. I knew how to come on like a thug.

"I'll call the police," he gasped.

"There's a policeman across the street," I said. "Go ahead and call him."

He looked hopefully over my shoulder. I made a lunge for him, grabbed his suit by the lapels, and tore the wallet out of his inside breast pocket.

"Give that back."

"One more peep out of you and I'll break your fucking

arm." I shoved him away and glanced through his wallet. It was a long, crocodile model for the busy executive, with laminated plastic infolds for photographs and credit cards. "Let's see," I said. "Floyd Connolly, born Boston, Massachusetts, August twelfth, nineteen fifty-three. You're awfully young for this kind of work, Floyd. That a picture of your girlfriend? So-so. Her eyes are too close together."

"You have no right . . ."

"Only two dollars in cash. But I guess with all those credit cards you don't need cash. State Congressional Library pass . . . State of California employee identification . . . U.S. Senate pass . . . *Richard Staples.*" I snapped the wallet shut. "Who the fuck are you?"

"You can read, can't you?"

"You work for Senator Staples?"

"What's it look like?" He twisted his chin up defensively. "What the hell are you following me for?"

"I was told to." He took off his glasses and began polishing them with the end of his striped tie.

"By the Senator?"

"Who else?"

I gave him his wallet back and stared at him, trying to make sense of it.

"How long have you worked for Staples?"

"Six months," he said breezily.

"I don't think I like you following me, Floyd."

"I was following the Senator's wife," he protested. "When you met her I started following you. It's nothing personal."

"Of course not. It isn't going to be anything personal when I give you a poke in the eye, either."

"Haw haw," he laughed weakly. "I wish you'd stop saying those things. I'm just doing my job."

"Following the Senator's wife isn't government work."

"I'm a junior aide. I have to do what I'm asked."

"Tell the Senator that if he wants to know something about me all he has to do is pick up a phone."

"I'll tell him anything you want." He had an earnest, humorless look on his face. "You don't have to threaten me with physical violence just because I'm doing my job." He smoothed out his tie and added complacently. "Anyway, I don't know what you're making a fuss about. The Senator knows."

"Knows what?"

"About you and his wife."

"Have you been peeking through keyholes, Floyd?"

"Oh, come on," he sniffed. "That's hardly necessary. We know who you are and what you do. Your intentions stick out a mile."

"What are you talking about?"

"Well," he sneered. "It's obvious you're hoping to compromise the Senator. I believe the legal term is blackmail."

Sexual assault, robbery, murder, and now blackmail—the list of charges against me was growing every day. Who did these people think I was? Was it inconceivable to them that I might actually be in love with the Senator's wife?

"You're a snide little shit, Floyd, you know that?"

"You can call me all the names you want," he said huffily, "but everyone knows what you're after, and it's just not going to work. The Senator wasn't born yesterday."

For some reason it infuriated me more that Staples believed I was trying to blackmail his wife than that the police thought I was guilty of murder. "You tell the Senator to meet me at three o'clock this afternoon. The Highland Fling. It's a bar on Fairfax. Have you got that?"

"Of course," he said. "I have a photographic memory."

"Good." I took his nose between my thumb and forefinger and gave it a good twist. "Remember *that* next time you stick it into my business."

17

By a quarter to three the lunchtime crowd at the Highland Fling had thinned out and I had the place almost to myself. It was dark and cool inside, and nearly silent except for the hum of the air conditioners and the click of pool balls coming from the back room. The bartender was counting the money in the till and humming softly to himself.

At about ten minutes to three two men in dark suits entered the bar. One of them took a seat by the door while the other one glanced into the back room. The one sitting down was fair-haired with a thick neck and broad shoulders. He had very bleached-looking skin and pale eyebrows and lashes. The other one gave me a slow probing glance on his way back to his seat. They both ordered Cokes and kept their suit jackets buttoned. They looked like cops or secret service men; the way they held themselves and talked to each other you could see they were on the job and not just grabbing a drink in the middle of the afternoon. For that matter, they could have been syndicate boys; all these lower-echelon corporate types tend toward the same style.

Close to three o'clock a third man came in and joined them. After a moment's huddled conversation he walked over to my table and sat down. He had a long sallow face with a heavy blue shadow around the jaw and upper lip. His eyes had the black oily shine of olives.

"Cole?"

"Yes."

"You're not wired, by any chance?"

I looked at him, puzzled.

"Bugged," he said.

I just looked at him, saying nothing.

He ran his hands under the table and examined the candle burning in a red glass bowl on the top, picking it up and inspecting its bottom. Then he took a small meter device out of his pocket and passed it over my body. It was about the size of a pack of cigarettes.

"You've got to be kidding," I said.

"You armed, Cole?" he asked in a soft gravelly voice.

"Just my tank," I said. "But I left it parked outside."

"You armed?" he repeated, holding my eyes.

"No, but the chair you're sitting on explodes when you stand up."

"We're armed," he said, without a trace of humor. He moved away to the back of the bar and took a seat by himself near the entrance to the men's room. One of the men at the other table got up and walked out and came back a moment later with the Senator. It was dead on three o'clock.

Staples had got into the cloak-and-dagger spirit, too. He was dressed in a loudly patterned tweed sports jacket with an open-collar shirt and pale gray slacks. Large dark glasses hid most of his face and his blond hair was concealed by a snap-brim Panama with a black band. With the shades and the hat tilted low on his forehead he could have been a bookie or some variety of racetrack dandy.

He bought a drink at the bar and then with a casual

glance around the room came over and joined me. He removed his hat and took off the sunglasses. He was not quite as young as I'd remembered. There was something of the aging actor about his looks, a wornout glamor which you see in carefully preserved older women and homosexuals in their fifties. The blond hair didn't quite ring true; the teeth were too aggressively perfect. It was a look I disliked in men; for it made me anxious for their dignity, unwillingly conscious of all the telltale signs where their age showed through the carefully maintained illusion of youth. I'd always seen Staples before in the public limelight, the golden-haired Senator with the hundred-watt smile. It was only now, when no trace of a smile was visible, that I saw his mouth was actually thin-lipped and rather brutally carved.

"I received your message, Mr. Cole," he said. "I thought I'd come see you in person."

"Do you always travel with that entourage?"

"When I'm dealing with certain types it seems advisable."

" 'Uneasy lies the head that wears a crown.' "

"I would have thought Shakespeare was hardly your line." His lip lifted in a faint sneer.

"Why don't you tell me what my line is, Senator?"

He stirred his drink with the plastic swizzle stick, took a sip, and patted his lips with the napkin which had printed on it, "Don't go away mad. Just go away."

"I have no interest in playing games, Cole," he said evenly. "I know what you are. Tell me what you want and we can terminate this meeting."

"What do you think I want?"

"I've had you researched." He waved his hand in dismissal. "I can't stop my wife from making a fool of herself but I can stop her from being blackmailed."

"You don't know what you're talking about."

"Don't I?" he grimaced. "Four days ago you murdered a woman in Hollywood for her jewels. I won't bother with the niceties of presumed innocence. The next night you saw my wife at a fund-raiser and subsequently seduced her. You did it for one reason and one reason alone: you think you can blackmail me into helping you get off the murder charge."

"Maybe that's what you'd like to believe."

"Is it? My wife asked me last night about the Ryman murder. It didn't make any sense until I heard you were the prime suspect."

"Have you discussed this with Michelle?" I asked.

It was a useless question. It didn't take much to see that Staples wasn't the kind of man to confide in his wife. His kind of man confided in no one. His response to a failing marriage was to have his wife followed, and when he uncovered a lover, to buy him off behind her back.

"You won't blackmail me," he said. "You can threaten to spread our names over every tabloid in the country, but I won't interfere in the legal process. You may think that kind of publicity would ruin my career. You're wrong. I'd eventually get the sympathy of the public. I'd come out stronger than before."

"You sound like you've already taken a Gallup poll."

"How much to get you out of my hair?" he snarled. "That's all I want to know."

"Not a dime, Senator. I'm seeing Michelle because I want to see her. I was seeing her before Julie Ryman was killed. That's what I wanted to tell you. I don't want anything from you except something you don't even care about—Michelle. I'm glad I met you. Now I understand why your wife could risk losing her marriage . . . there was nothing there to lose."

"Let me be even simpler." He leaned toward me. "You

live off the good graces of a small number of people—such as Mrs. Lautner. And the good graces of places like the Polo Lounge and Chasen's. The same goes for your clients. You're just a hanger-on. And unless you want to find another crowd to hang on to, you'd better not see my wife again."

"You can do better than that. Not being allowed into Chasen's isn't going to break my heart."

"I thought you were smart, Cole. I assumed at least you had the slimy cunning of your breed. I'll make it really simple for you. I have power in this town. I have influence with the police and the courts. I have influence in the appointment of judges. Do you understand me?"

"You'll go to any lengths, no matter how corrupt, to put me away. I think I've absorbed the gist of it."

"I've warned you." He rose to his feet. "I don't think you'd look so good in a wheelchair, Cole. Even to my wife. Think about it." He put his dark glasses on, yanked the hat down hard on his head and swept out of the bar with his aides and bodyguard bringing up the rear.

It was only after he was gone that I noticed my hands were trembling. I'd tried to maintain an insolent, unworried composure throughout the interview but the instant it was over I felt like I'd been clubbed. There was really nothing to feel confident about. A man like Staples had friends, powerful friends, legitimate and otherwise. It would take a word dropped in a certain quarter, a veiled hint, and soon after I might be met in an alley, or a car would fail to brake as I crossed a street. Was I exaggerating? Giving way to paranoia? Was it after all a respectable world out there? No, the country was organized along lines of interest and influence from the Senate through local government into the police department and the courts. Nor did these lines of influence end there, but went deeper until they could no longer be judged or opposed, being illegitimate at the root.

18

I waited until much later that evening to try and find Leroy. It turned out to be harder than I expected. His working hours were nighttime; his office was his limousine and a dozen clubs, bars, steam baths, and gay dance palaces. I tried Studio One and learned I'd missed him by half an hour. He turned out to be expected at the Athenian Baths where I ended up waiting an hour for him without success. Everywhere I went I found people who had seen Leroy or were waiting to see him. It was one of his habits to give out his schedule for the night and then play a subtle variation on it. He was like some dictator afraid of political assassination. He didn't like the world to be able to count on him definitely being anywhere at any time. He was dealing coke that night, holding large sums of money that belonged to other people, buying heavily, making drops, all the while keeping up his normal round, procuring boys for clients and making his collections. If I didn't see him, I felt his influence everywhere: an aged queen waiting in a bar for a boy in Leroy's stable, a group at the baths waiting for reds and cocaine, a young junkie hustler hoping to get on Leroy's books.

By the time I'd made the rounds once, I could be almost sure that Leroy knew I was searching for him.

I drove on, cruising Highland, Hollywood Boulevard, Selma, and all the little streets in between. The stores and restaurants were closed; the theatergoers and tourists had gone home. Now the streets belonged to their nocturnal denizens: the hustlers, pimps, hookers, transvestites and slowly moving patrol cars. It was a scene played out on the street corners and in the shadows of vacant lots. Young watchful faces of boys loomed in my headlights, trying to look through my windshield to see what I was like. They were spaced every ten yards or so, hands on their hips, or thumbs hooked into their belts, or draped around street lamps, or just sitting on the curb with their faces in their hands. Each one, by his clothing and stance, signaled his particular type: there were provocative, girlish boys, flighty coquettes interspersed with brooding neo-James Deans, weight lifters, blond beachboys, macho bikers. There were pros and amateurs, expensively dressed ones and ragged-looking kids in scuffed tennis shoes and grimy T-shirts; the runaways of fifteen and sixteen willing to do anything for a meal and a bed for the night. There were the slightly older adolescents, hollow-eyed, strung-out, with wasted bodies and dyed gold hair; the motorcycle heavies in black boots and sleeveless denim jackets, defiantly tattooed, bristling with chains and studs. Cruising slowly, men in cars examined the human goods for sale, slowed down, speeded up, halted to bargain. And then these streets gave way to others with cracked deserted pavements and parked cars inside which men strained at each other's flesh for what flesh could give in the way of relief, solace, peace from the burdens of the night. Decadence California-style—fuelled on reds, coke,

angel dust, booze, bennies, junk, poppers—anything that
could alter the pain of what you were.

I sipped the pint of vodka from my glove compartment
and cruised on. In that neighborhood at that hour of the
night you had to be a stone not to feel the waves of despair
that had washed up this tide of human flotsam. If there was
such a thing as an apocalypse you knew it had already happened. The streets of the Hollywood Tenderloin could have
been the back alleys of Rome at the fall of the Empire: dim
torch-lit passages choked with suffering, corrupt humanity,
human slavery at a premium, any perversion or luxury for
sale.

I finally spotted Leroy's Continental parked in front of the
Paradise Ball Room on Highland. It had been freshly waxed
and gleamed beautifully under the street light but someone
had snapped the telephone aerial off and raked the paint off
the side doors. That happened a lot. Kids spray-painted
windshields and slashed tires, anyone's tires, impersonally.
In the summer especially you could feel the rage simmering
below the surface of the city, ready to fasten on any object
whether it was a beautiful car or an old woman who could
be robbed of her food stamps.

The Paradise Ball Room was packed with men, crowding
the dance floor and lined up three deep at the bar. Throbbing out of the speakers, Martha and the Vandellas' "Heat
Wave" did battle with the lurching swell of conversation.
There is nothing quite comparable in the straight world to
the heavy passion and paranoia of a gay bar toward closing
time. It was the hour of the night when the pairing off
quickens in speed, the drinking gets more destructive, the
desperation starts to leak out. The room was jammed, elbow
to elbow, buttock to buttock, with short-haired young men
in jeans and T-shirts, talking and drinking furiously, their

eyes constantly straying, inviting and disdaining advances, assessing and being assessed. A sign above the bar warned, "Flies attract germs. So keep yours closed." In the darker alcoves, lost in the bedlam of anonymous bodies, strangers caressed each other, kneeled to each other.

I shouldered my way through the press of dancers, drawing hostile stares, and inquiring glances. The homosexual ego is stretched closer to breaking point; at the hint of rejection it snaps more quickly into disdain. It is all done through the eyes: the eyes ask a question—"Are you interested?"—and you either blankly veil your eyes or show an answering light. I had drunk a lot and I was looking for Leroy and I wasn't interested in soothing egos. I could feel the faint waves of paranoia and enmity I created as I moved toward the bar.

"Hello, Julian." A hand closed on my arm and when I turned I saw Teddy Lime. He was vaguely dancing with an older man in a Hawaiian shirt, shuffling spasmodically, his eyes barely able to stay open. His white suit was stained with wine, his shirt stuck to his chest by perspiration.

"Get you your money," he slurred. "Tomorrow. Just got to earn it." He inclined his head toward his dancing partner who glared frostily at me.

"There's no rush, Teddy."

"Not my scene at all, man," he said. "Doing a favor for Leroy. You know Leroy? Faggot pimp? Mr. Low Life? He's going to get me some straight tricks after tonight. Got to prove myself with fatso here." He laughed softly to himself. "Most distasteful, old boy. Not my style at all. I was always a ladies' man . . ." He smiled lazily, asleep on his feet, mumbling in an imitation of an English accent. "Always abhorred buggery. A mere temporary stopgap, old boy, to pay the rent."

"Where's Leroy?" I shouted to be heard above the din of music and conversation.

"Ah, Leroy." Teddy draped an arm around my shoulder. "The man we all come to, Our Father in Heaven, the Great Leroy. Are you also Leroy's creature, friend? I thought you were Anne's darling boy, the man of the hour? No? A mere pansy after all? Pity, that. Great pity. . . ."

"Are you dancing with me or not?" Teddy's friend in the Hawaiian shirt put his hands on his hips and sulked. "I mean, make up your mind, darling. You're not the only fish in the sea. . . ."

"With you!" Teddy lifted his hands to his partner. "I'm yours, all yours. Do with me as you will." Out of the corner of his mouth, he said to me, "Leroy's out back, showing off a new boy."

I elbowed my way out of the room into the back patio where food was being served and the air was fresher. Leroy was leaning on his own against an ivy-covered wall beneath an orange spot which gave him a slightly translucent, hideous glow. He was dressed in a pale lilac suit and a white silk shirt with ruffled front and cuffs. A bright green silk scarf concealed his long neck. The brim of a white Borsalino was tipped rakishly low over his forehead and he was smoking a spectacularly carved amber yellow Meerschaum. From his glassy fixed eyes and tight-locked jaw I could see he was wired high on coke.

"Lookin' good, Julie." He made a serpentine shimmy with his hips and slapped my open palm. "Lookin' *good*."

"I've been trying to find you."

"I hear you, brother." He nodded rhythmically, gazing straight ahead at something behind me. "All night long the drums been saying the same message—'Julian's coming.'"

"Come on, Leroy, I got to talk to you in private."

"It's cool here. No one can hear nothing in this racket."

"This is important, damn it."

"Dig, man," he said. "I may look like I'm just standing against this wall playing with myself but I'm working. I got to keep my eye on something."

"I heard you were showing off a new boy."

"Gotta make sure none of these fruits steal him off me," he sniffed, wiping his nose with the back of his hand. "You want some evil cocaine, man, I got it. Make you feel like the coldest prettiest snowflake in the world."

"The hell with cocaine. What about the Ryman killing?"

"Don't talk to me about that shit." He sighed. "That's all I been hearing about. Fucking cops been on my ass like glue."

"Yeah, well I've been getting the third degree."

"When you get the third degree, sucker, you know about it. You walkin' around, you got money in your pocket, that ain't no third degree. What's the matter, they ask you a few questions? They've been kicking ass all over town the last few days."

"It's not that simple," I said. "I was with a trick that night but she won't cop to having been with me."

"I told you none of that rich pussy was any good." He shrugged.

"You take this awfully cool, Leroy. You sent me to the Rymans. You jived me on the whole thing. I'm telling you I need some help."

"Oh yeah?" He wasn't even paying attention.

"You know what I think, Leroy?"

"What?" His eyes stayed fixed on something across the room.

"I think you're playing games with me. And you know what? I think I'm going to put you in the fucking hospital."

"Say what!" His head jerked around. "Hey, be cool. I didn't know you had the heat on so bad."

"I need an alibi. I've got cops following me everywhere. My hotel is staked out."

"I hear you," he said. "We'll fix something tight for you. But just lighten up on that violent talk. Like what *is* that? Violence, man, like violence is *nowhere*. The cops is just running everyone's ass ragged 'cause they haven't got anything."

"They've got me. They think I'm Jack the Ripper."

"Yeah, well they never did catch old Jack, did they?" He chuckled. "If I was a cop I'd be more interested in Ryman himself—that's a freak."

"But he's got an alibi."

"It's probably as phony as yours is gonna be." Leroy leaned over to me. "Step into the john, brother. I'll turn you on to something that'll clear your head. I got a thing later on tonight I'll let you in on. Two hundred dollars."

The crowd in the main room was migrating out onto the patio. A sea of bodies pressed us back against the wall.

"I'm through doing your shit, Leroy."

"A little distraction be good for you," he crooned.

"Through with creep acts. I'm finished with it. This whole scene. I don't want to know anymore." I hadn't thought about what I was saying, or even known I was going to say it. The words seemed to come out perfectly formed, a decision: I was retiring. The second I'd said it, I knew it was right. It was purest impulse but sometimes that's the only way of regaining possession of yourself, like heaven which has to be taken by storm. I wanted out. I had wanted out for a long time and been afraid to admit it to myself.

"I heard about your other problems, too," Leroy said casually.

"What problems?"

"Your clients, Julie. Your rich pussy. They're looking for new boys. The cops have made you too hot. They won't touch you. Ask around. . . ."

"I guess you didn't hear me," I said. "I'm through doing tricks. For good."

"Hey, Julie, you ask me to help you out of a tight spot. I'm glad to fix you up an alibi. But then you tell me you won't do my tricks. How you expect me to help you out?"

There it was, I thought, the bottom line. They didn't let you quit. You were to be kept in harness until you were all used up. At the end of the line was drug addiction as in Teddy Lime's case, the terminal jobs for fags, and then the boneyard. I needed an alibi, Teddy needed a shot; neither of us was going to get what we wanted without paying hard coin.

"Put it this way, Leroy," I said. "You got me in the tight spot. If I go down on this one, you're just gonna be one more street nigger who made it to Folsom. You hear me?"

"Why you bad-mouthing me?" he cried. "You'll get your alibi. How am I supposed to know you're through doing tricks? I was trying to hustle myself a little business."

"I'll tell the cops everything, Leroy." I smiled full in his face. "Enough to put you away for a long time."

"I'm getting you the fucking alibi," he said furiously. "You got it. Would you stop talking about the goddamn police!"

"Sure, Leroy. I just wanted to clear the air. I'll be seeing you around." This time he didn't offer me his hand, or go through any of his superdude-routine, and I didn't offer him mine. He'd said violence was nowhere, but in the end it was the only thing he respected.

19

In my dreams that night a seething tableau of lividly grotesque faces laughed and mocked me. I remember moving through the rooms of a smoky, labyrinthine cellar filled with dwarfs, obese women, cackling queens, snarling dogs, and pale, narcissistic couples with dreamy, remote faces full of cruelty and disdain. An icy black shadow followed me through the warren of rooms, breathing over my shoulder in a dry obscene wheeze. It lurked at the edge of my field of vision. I started to run and it suddenly sprang at my face. It was wizened and black like a charred human skeleton and it held a rake lifted to strike at me. I screamed and woke up with my chest heaving as if I'd been suffocated. It was already light outside. I threw open the windows and breathed in the already warm air. The low summer sky was washed with pastel tints of chemical waste; the city lay prostrate under a sun that had risen but remained invisible behind its cover of smog. Normally the birds sang loudly in the morning but the courtyard was silent. I could still feel the alcohol in my blood from the night before, throbbing around my eyes and temples. After drinking several glasses of ice water I lay down on the couch and went back to sleep.

The smell of smoke awoke me. It was a smell you associated with another season and another part of the country: the hint of wood burning in a distant snowbound field. I sat up and looked around the room. Papers from my desk were scattered over the floor and the curtains were flapping and blowing in front of the open windows. The air coming into the room was hot with a sandpaper edge to it that seemed to rub unpleasantly on the nerves. Outside the window the air was a jaundiced yellow, full of flying ash and dirt particles and twigs. It was the first Santa Ana wind of the year—late summer winds that boil up in the heat of the desert and come whistling down the canyons in fiery blasts. But there was more to it than that. I turned on the radio and got a news flash: fires had broken out in the Santa Monica Mountains and were jumping from ridge to ridge. At the summits of the peaks the wind speed was already in excess of sixty miles per hour. A rain of ash like a black snowfall was floating down over the city. Drivers were being asked to use their headlights in broad daylight.

Looking down into the hotel courtyard I saw the small swimming pool had turned gray; the plants and white flagstone paths, the deck chairs and tables were all covered in a fine charcoal soot. Some of the descending particles were the size of curls and ribbons of burned newspaper. But it was the light that was the strangest thing: such an unearthly yellow light, it seemed to belong to another landscape and period of time. You half expected to see dinosaurs lumbering through it and giant flying lizards beating the air with their wings.

I rubbed my eyes. My whole body was hot, itching, and subtly irritated. It was the kind of weather where your nerves cry out for rain but you know for a certainty it won't come. There was a terrible pent-up pressure in the air, a

damp, building gloom to the atmosphere. The phone rang
and I picked it up and waited for Miss Breame to go off the
line.

"Thank you, Miss Breame," I finally said.

There was a short click and then Sunday's voice came
through, slightly obscured by a background hum of voices
and typewriters.

"I hope I didn't wake you, Julian," he said. "I hear you
had quite a night. Jarvis tells me you really did the rounds."

"I don't know who Jarvis is."

"Jarvis is the guy assigned to you nights. He says he
nearly got raped by a giant fruit in the men's room at the
Paradise Ball Room."

"You're in a good mood, Sunday," I said. "What's the bad
news?"

"Now that's a hangover talking," he said easily. "You
don't really mean that."

"I mean, what's on your mind?"

"I didn't get much sleep either," he said. "I was up most
of the night reading. You've had quite a life, Julian. You really kept a detailed record. All those women in your diary
would be very nervous if they knew what you'd written
about them. It's the kind of thing you could sell. . . ."

I couldn't bring myself to speak; he had a huge advantage
over me, being in possession of the diaries.

"Why the change of name, Julian?" he asked. "Chris-
topher March not classy enough for you? It's an unusual career for a boy from Sandstone Falls, Iowa. You were what
they call an army brat. Your father was a corporal stationed
overseas. I guess that's how you learned your languages.
You ran away from home six times and lied about your age
to join the Navy at sixteen. Your father traced you, brought
you back . . ."

"He also put me up for adoption when I was five. He was also a drunk. He was also a sadist."

"You didn't keep a diary in those days, kid."

"The orphanages I grew up in didn't encourage it. Have you got a point you're aiming at, Sunday, or is this just your way of amusing yourself?"

"You rejoined the Navy at eighteen, got out on a medical discharge a year later. You went to school in France, then two years working as a purser for an airline. Fired for missing too many planes. From there you worked cruise ships as an entertainment director. You've done a lot of traveling."

"That's right."

"You were arrested in New York on a smuggling charge. Trying to bring an antique violin into the States from Paris."

"It was a favor for a friend. I didn't know it was valuable. I wasn't convicted. My friend owned up and paid the duty."

"You roughed up a guy yesterday on Westwood Boulevard. Had yourself a little scuffle. He was following you."

"I didn't notice."

"Later in the day you had a meet with some syndicate people. They were in a rented car. We're trying to find out who they are."

Sunday's imagination appeared to be taking flight, weaving some melodramatic fantasy, though the Senator's clandestine behavior did smack of organized crime.

"Anyway, it isn't all clear yet, but we'll get there. All that traveling you've done, working for the airline, the boats, the smuggling charge, the connection with an L.A. pusher. I think you were a drug courier for some outfit. I think you got contacts with some big hoods. I think you're trying to set up a route out of the country. I think you better come in this afternoon at three o'clock and let us put you in a lineup."

"You've been watching too much television," I said.

"I like to think big," he said. "Three o'clock, Casanova." The line went dead. The last time he'd got me away from my room it had been a decoy to search it. I wondered what he had in mind this time. Did he seriously believe any of the things he'd told me? Or was it just more of his Kafkaesque technique to sow panic and confusion?

I should have showered and shaved and changed my clothes but I didn't seem to have any energy. I just sat in an armchair by the window and watched the black ash coming down through the yellow sky, smoked cigarettes, and agonized over what I ought to do. I must have dozed off because the next thing I knew I was awakened by a pounding on the door and the sound of my name being called. It was Michelle.

I bolted out of the chair, flew across the room and threw open the door. There she was, looking quite small and almost plain in tennis shoes and jeans and a faded T-shirt. She was wearing no makeup and her eyes looked faintly blood-shot and worn. For some reason this made her seem all the more precious to me but when I embraced her she merely sagged listlessly in my arms. When I tried to kiss her mouth she turned her face into my chest and sighed unhappily.

"What's the matter, baby? You look completely worn out."

"I didn't get much sleep." She disengaged herself and walked slowly into the center of the room and looked around. She let her handbag drop to the floor, then hugged herself, as if she were cold. I'd never seen her behave like this and couldn't figure out what was the matter. Still, the sight of her had given me new energy; and at least I knew that I had some good news for her. I made her sit down on the couch and warmed her hands between mine.

"I've been thinking about what you said the other day," I said eagerly. "I think you're right. I really do want to change. I've decided to . . ."

"Don't say anything, Julian." She pulled her hands free, tears suddenly filling her eyes.

"What do you mean?"

"I can't bear to hear it."

"How do you know what I'm going to say?" I stared at her, baffled by this apparently altered Michelle. Somewhere deep down, before she spoke, though, I think I knew that the worst had happened.

"Julian," she sobbed. "I made Rick a promise. That's what I came to tell you. I'm going to Rome for two months. It's the least I can do for him. He believes it'll give me some perspective. I don't want to go but I can't just wreck his life."

I sat back on the couch and let the air out of my lungs very slowly. I felt like I'd been hammered hard in the center of the chest; my stomach was alive with a weak aching vulnerability. It was somehow what I'd always feared and unconsciously expected: it had been for a good reason that I'd always avoided falling in love. I'd never believed I'd actually get the one thing I craved most in life. Now I'd been led into wanting it, needing it, and it was being taken away from me.

"Will you wait for me?" she pleaded.

"When are you leaving?"

"Next Monday."

I remember the room was abnormally dark, filled with the whoosh and crack of the curtains billowing in the hot wind.

"Will we see each other before you leave?" I knew how to mask my feelings: my question was posed with a kind of casual affection as if she was a friend whose welfare interested me.

"I don't know if I could stand it." She burst into sobs and groped blindly for her handbag, rummaging for tissues.

"I don't know," I said with that sensation of unreality you feel when you agree with something that is going to make you unhappy for the rest of your life. "You're probably right. There's a lot at stake. It's better this way."

She lifted her face to me, with a trace of horror in her eyes. Her skin was so translucently pale I could see a wash of freckles over the bridge of her nose and cheeks which I'd never noticed before.

"I have to know if you'll wait," she whispered.

"Where I'm probably going, Michelle, that's the only thing they let you do—wait."

"I've talked to Rick about that." She paused and looked at me to see how I was taking it. "He's going to try and help you. He knows you're innocent."

I could have told her I'd seen her husband and he wasn't about to do anything, but what was the point?

"I don't want his help," I shrugged. "We'll just have to see how it all turns out." I knew I didn't really have any right to ask anything of her or expect her to get involved in my life just as it was breaking to pieces. Still, the news of her imminent departure brought me very low. I'd believed she would stick with me. It was pretty hard to take and I felt that everything was running against me, for in a way my decision to quit being a gigolo was because of her. But I didn't tell her that. It hadn't been her pity that I wanted when I first started liking her, and I was determined to live without it now.

20

When I asked for Sunday the desk sergeant called over a young policeman who escorted me to a tiny cubicle at the end of the hall and told me to wait inside. There was a wooden bench, a bare electric bulb, and another door that was closed. There was not enough room to sit on the bench without your knees hitting the wall. I smoked a cigarette and then another and by then the air was so bad I had to open the other door. It gave onto a large high-ceilinged room divided into sections by wire-mesh screens. At the far end there was a desk for fingerprinting suspects and a curtained-off enclosure where mug shots were taken. Directly in front of me a young Mexican stood in front of a high desk, slowly removing all his clothes and leaving them in a pile on the floor. A plainclothes police officer then gave him a body search. The Mexican was made to open his mouth, bare his arm pits, lift the soles of his feet, and finally bend over and spread the cheeks of his buttocks. Groups of policemen moved in and out of the room, carrying files and escorting suspects from one part of the station to another. The Mexican's body looked pale and undernourished in the harsh electric light, his nudity almost surreal among the dark blue uniforms. His skin was milky-white except for his face, forearms, and a dark sunburned V at the throat.

Time passed slowly and I could feel a kind of claustrophobic panic trying to get a hold on me. Between the pale green walls of the cubicle I found it hard to breathe easily but I was afraid to move into the larger room. Sounds echoed sharply—the jangle of keys, iron doors clanging shut, typewriters and telexes and police radios all chattering. A steady stream of suspects was being processed through the room, mainly blacks and Chicanos, with the occasional white derelict. One man was brought in by brute force, a young, expensively dressed guy with a purple-and-black bruise swelling the side of his face. He was very drunk but looked like a guy who might be a successful Beverly Hills real estate agent, or the owner of a business. As he was led handcuffed into the room, he was spitting out abuse at the two officers holding his arms. I gathered they had had something to do with the bruise on his face. He kept yelling about his brother-in-law who was a lawyer and how the police would eat crow when they found out who they'd manhandled. His curses and threats continued as he unwillingly stripped off his clothes, growing weaker as he got down to his underpants. His noisy performance had drawn a crowd from the adjoining rooms. He didn't want to take his underpants off. Suddenly the fight went out of him and he began weeping but the policemen paid no more attention to his tears than to his threats.

The ordeal of stripping in front of the police silently and profoundly affected everyone I saw that day. It was more effective than any physical beating, attacking you at your most vulnerable point. The business of having to bend over and bear your ass to the scrutiny of a stranger was the coup de grâce. It was what you'd had to do for your mother in childhood. Now symbolically and literally it was driven home to you that your ass belonged to the police. You could shout and mouth off all you wanted; nothing changed the fact that they now controlled your body and that was all that counted.

It didn't take much imagination to see how I'd get on in prison. I didn't have the street savvy or survival skills to exist unharmed in that world. Other men would forcibly try and use me as a woman and if I resisted an individual protector, I'd be vulnerable to gang rape with a razor blade at my throat. The punishment would not be so much the denial of a free life outside as the imposition of the nightmare existence of prison.

I didn't know whether I'd been forgotten, or Sunday had purposefully let me cool my heels so that I might have just such sobering intimations of what lay in wait for me. Whatever, by the time someone collected me for the lineup I was well loaded with dread and nervous fright.

The waiting room for the lineup was in the basement. I was the last to arrive and I got the impression the six other men had been held there for some time before my arrival. Four of them were dark-haired, blue-eyed men of my age and build, though none of them looked at all like me. The other two were fair-haired and middle-aged. We weren't allowed to speak to each other. Large white numbered cards were hung around our necks and we were herded through a door onto a platform mounted at the end of a darkened room. A battery of lights was turned on us. A voice from a wall speaker said,

"All right, boys, stand full face please."

I was in the center of the line, number four.

"They gave us the bad spot," the guy next to me grumbled.

"What do you mean?"

"Witnesses always tend to pick out the guy in the middle. That's where the pigs put the guy they want identified."

We were made to slowly turn around and then walk a few steps forward and back like an unwilling chorus line. Cigarettes glowed in the darkness beyond the stage and occasionally a face suggested itself around a burning ember and vanished again.

"All right, boys, that'll be all," the voice said, then added, "don't call us. We'll call you." He didn't get any laughs.

A bluebottle fly was crawling up the wall behind Sunday's desk toward the light switch. Just before it reached the plastic fitting it flew off with an angry buzz to its original position on the door frame. Then it started its slow crawling approach all over again. It was a small office without windows. Two metal desks faced each other with a chair in between set against the wall where a *Playboy* pinup calendar hung. That's where I was sitting, the back of my head leaning against Miss August's silicone-enlarged breasts. Dirty yellow linoleum covered the floor. Sunday occupied one desk, his feet up, his hands folded loosely over his stomach. A cigarette burned in the corner of his mouth, a thin stream of blue smoke slanting across his face which was contorted in irritation. Perched on the edge of the other desk was a tall red-haired cop with a rakish ginger moustache and smooth, fiercely sculpted features. He had slanted green eyes, a hawkish nose, and deeply pocked skin. He was dressed in a loud plaid knit suit, a pink nylon shirt, a red tie, and yellow Earth shoes. He was deeply involved in shooting paper clips with a rubber band at the fly on the wall. His name was Curtiss and Sunday had told me he was in charge of the Ryman case. So far he hadn't said a word.

"You've been identified, Julian," Sunday said gravely.

"Who? Who could possibly identify me?"

He reached across the desk and picked up a typewritten sheet of paper from his IN tray. He spoke very slowly. "The Japanese motel clerk identifies you on both nights. You parked your blue Mercedes 450 SL about a half a block from the motel around ten o'clock the night of the murder. Then you proceeded up the block, turned into the motel, and entered."

"Who says this?"

"The guy who runs the porn-mill across the street from the Taj Mahal. He saw you, Julian."

"Sure, him and the Pope."

"Curtiss is Catholic. Leave the Pope out of it."

"First of all, that old Jap is nearly blind. He couldn't pick his own face out if you stuck him in front of a mirror. Second . . ." I tried to get the strangled sound out of my voice, "I wasn't there the night of the twenty-second. Why is this guy inventing all this?"

"He picked you out." Sunday shrugged.

"Both nights." Curtiss swung himself around to face me.

"Why?" I couldn't believe it. "Why would he do that?"

"Maybe because it's true." Sunday began tearing the cellophane off a fresh pack of cigarettes.

"Maybe he doesn't even understand what the hell he's doing," I said heatedly. "Anyway, what good is a witness like that? A guy who's nearly blind?"

"Looking ahead to the trial, Julian?" Sunday smiled mockingly.

"Two can play this game," I said. "Los Angeles is full of Mercedes."

"Convertibles?" Sunday asked. "Dark blue?"

"At night it would just look dark. It could be any number of colors. What was the license number?"

"The guy didn't see it," Sunday said shortly.

"You're damn right he didn't. There's no porn-mill across from the Taj Mahal. The whole block's dark."

There was a silence, finally broken by the sound of another paper clip striking the wall. Curtiss pinched the corner of his moustache and sniffed. "How'd you feel when you went back and checked, Julian?"

"You must be pretty hard up to try this kind of crap." It was starting to occur to me that they had lied about the Japanese clerk's identification as well. "What's next?" I said. "Am I meant to break down and confess?"

Sunday kept his eyes on me while he opened a desk drawer and removed a large manila envelope. Inside were six fifty-dollar bills encased in a clear plastic envelope and a stained monogrammed paper envelope which he shook out on to the desk.

"Recognize these?"

I shook my head.

"They were found under your mattress." Sunday's voice slowed down with a deceptive laziness. "The envelope we found them in is covered in Julie Ryman's fingerprints. The fingerprints were easy to identify. They were smeared in blood. Want to know something else? There's a pair of your trousers and underpants at the lab. The chemists have found traces of Julie Ryman's blood on them, too."

It was like a nightmare. If they kept pulling out things like that I'd start to believe myself that I'd killed her.

"I told you it got heavy the night I was there. She was . . . clawing herself. I told you that. I've never seen that money in my life."

"It must have flown through your window and hid under the bed," Curtiss yawned.

"Didn't you ever wonder why a supposed murderer would keep a monogrammed envelope stolen from his alleged victim under his mattress? What next, Sunday? I suppose you found her jewels, too. Where were they? Sitting on the piano?"

"Shut up," Sunday barked. "Every guilty person always gives you a million logical reasons why he couldn't have done something. Sure you'd have to have a screw loose to leave important evidence lying around. Murderers aren't logical. They set themselves up."

"Someone is setting *me* up," I cried. "Can't you see that?"

"The possibility occurred to me," he grunted.

"What about Ryman himself?" I said. "This sounds like something kinky he might get into."

Curtiss stood up and removed his suit jacket and then edged down the top of the desk until he was almost sitting in my lap. "Twenty Beverly Hills businessmen say different. Ryman's a distinguished veteran. He's an active Republican. He's got an alibi made out of ferroconcrete."

"Apart from a harmless taste for watching other men screw and assault his wife, I'm sure he's a credit to the community."

"Assaulting people can be fun." He measured me with his eyes. "I think you were at the Taj Mahal the night of the twenty-second. I think you're guilty as sin. I think you went over to the motel, did a trick, played some rough games, got stupid, or drunk, or greedy, beat her up, stole her jewels and money, and then raped her afterwards. I think you're going to get the death penalty. I think as soon as we get rid of our pious faggot governor, all the scumbags on Death Row are going to get the electric chair, and you'll be one of them. I think if I bounced you off the walls you'd confess."

The air in the office was hot and low on oxygen. A spicy, sweaty smell came off Curtiss in waves.

"If you're so sure I'm guilty," I said, "then arrest me so I can get a lawyer."

Sunday blew some smoke and waved it away from his face.

"We think you're guilty but we're not going to recommend your arrest," he said. "We don't have enough evidence yet. Anyway, you're easy to find."

"If you are being framed," Curtiss said, "you can do us and yourself more good on the street."

"I think you guys know damn well someone planted that money under my bed." I looked from one to the other. "You could have put a giraffe in the middle of that lineup and the Jap would have picked it out. I think you know Ryman is a bug but you're afraid to make waves just like you're afraid to get the truth out of Lisa Williams and her husband. I don't think it bothers you a hell of a lot if the wrong guy goes down for this, that's what I think."

"Thinking may not be your strong point, kid." Sunday got up.

"Can I go now?"

"One other thing, Julian," he said. "A guy like you doesn't wear well in the joint. The other cons are going to take it out of your ass. We can fix it so you're protected inside, or just let things take their normal, ugly course. Next time you feel like mouthing off, remember that. We may not look like much but right now the police are about all you've got."

21

I was waiting for the elevator up from the underground garage of my hotel when I saw a movement in the shadows near the entrance ramp. Or did I? I couldn't trust my senses anymore. Just driving back from the police station I'd nearly had three accidents because I'd kept looking in my rearview mirror instead of watching the traffic ahead. I pushed the elevator button again. I could hear voices coming down the shaft as someone held the door and conversed on the floor above.

Again, out of the periphery of my vision I sensed a movement across the garage: a glint of yellow and white in the shadows cast by one of the concrete pillars. Something familiar and ice-cold seemed to brush the back of my neck.

I should have run directly across the garage but I was afraid. I banged the elevator button and kicked the door. I heard a car door slam, an engine roar into life, and then a dark brown Porsche convertible reversed out from behind the pillar and turned up the ramp leading on to Wilshire Boulevard. The driver had short blond hair with a dyed look. I didn't get a look at his face and his license plates were too dusty to read. Maybe he was just a tenant or visitor getting into his car. He had driven out quite slowly, with no appearance of haste.

Miss Breame had said I'd had a blond visitor shortly before the police searched my room and found the money under my mattress. But the city was full of young men with blond hair. I must have seen a hundred last night alone.

I walked over to where the Porsche had been parked and studied the ground. The concrete floor was stained with oil slicks. There was a litter of cigarette butts and ash where someone had emptied a car ashtray. Did these things mean anything at all? Was I being paranoid, inventing danger where it didn't exist?

The first thing I did when I got back to my room was to search it. I went through everything systematically as the police had done but all I found was a tiny vial of French perfume under the sofa cushions. It was Michelle's scent which was the last thing I wanted to think about. How could I have been so naive as to let myself fall in love with the wife of a United States senator? Or imagine that she would give up Staples to stake her future on a gigolo accused of murder? I could see it pretty clearly from her side, women being much like men in the way they divide the opposite sex into the ones you fool around with and the ones you marry. I was the "other man" and nothing I could do would change it.

If I hadn't had a murder charge hanging over me, perhaps I wouldn't have taken Michelle's change of heart so badly. If I hadn't felt so inwardly drained by the destruction of my hopes, I might have been able to think clearly about the murder charge. Between the two worries, I became almost incapable of doing anything to help myself. I was fighting to save my life and simultaneously the only thing I loved in life had been taken from me.

I should have been stronger, not given in to depression. But that's as meaningless as saying I should have been a nuclear physicist instead of a gigolo. What I did was to get drunk. I just lay on the couch and drank Scotch neat from the bottle and stared at the ceiling. It had been a waste of time, I thought, to search my room because whoever had planted the money wasn't dumb enough to believe he could keep sticking bits of material evidence into my living quarters. He would have to change his tactics. The murder weapon and Julie Ryman's jewelry were probably still in his possession. I tried to put myself into the position of the person trying to frame me and took another swig from the bottle. The logical next move would be to leave some further evidence somewhere in the hotel, bury it in the garden, stash it in the trash, hide it in the laundry room, or even simpler just stick it in my car.

Sunday had said it—"Thinking may not be your strong point, kid"—and I was beginning to think he was right. If the blond boy in the garage had been waiting for me to come back, what was he doing now? He wasn't lying on his back drinking and feeling sorry for himself.

My car didn't look like it had been touched but then Blondie wasn't likely to have left dotted lines and arrows pointing to what he'd done. I'd left it unlocked. The beige leather interior still had that new-car smell, the dashboard clock was still keeping time, the radio still worked when you pushed the button. What would happen if I turned on the ignition? Would I be blown to bits by a bomb?

I didn't know whether I was scaring myself on purpose, or actually making a useful attempt to check out every possibility. The whiskey only heightened this sense of unreality.

I opened the hood and peered at the engine and stuck my hands down inside the wires and pipes. I didn't know a bomb from a carburetor. Any of the wires I saw could have always been there or could have been rigged in the last hour. I looked in the trunk, removed the mat, the spare tire and tool kit. Inside the car, I emptied the contents of the ashtray, glove compartment, console, and door pockets. I yanked out the floor mats, ripped back the carpeting, unscrewed the seat cushions. I was pouring with sweat. I took a deep breath and started the car and waited for the explosion. It wasn't forthcoming. I tried the air conditioning, windshield wipers, heater, and automatic gizmo for raising and lowering the convertible roof. Everything worked perfectly. I felt like going through my pockets and emptying my shoes in case someone had planted the murder weapon on me while I wasn't looking. Actually I felt like checking myself into a closed psychiatric ward for some electroshock therapy. What I was doing was absurd, a mere exercise in paranoia.

I was convinced the blond guy had just been innocently getting into his Porsche to drive away as millions of people do every day in the city when they want to get from one place to another. But I got my flashlight anyway and slid under the car and rolled around in an oil slick and got my hands good and dirty feeling around the shocks and chassis. I saw various wires, fuse boxes, and pipes whose functions I couldn't fathom. Oily red transmission fluid dripped onto my forehead and ran into my eye; dust and soot, loosened by my fingers, cascaded down on me. I turned and cut my shoulder against something hard and sharp.

The last thing I did was pop the hubcaps off. It was the last thing because when the third polished chrome disc clattered to the ground and stopped wobbling I saw a gray felt bag was fixed to its interior with black electrician's tape.

The initials on the bag were J. R., and inside were two di-

amond bracelets, a gold wedding ring, and a mourning
brooch with a lock of brown hair barely visible through the
oval glass. The lock of hair was mounted on red velvet, the
heart-shaped brooch itself framed in dark antique silver.
Whose hair was it, I wondered? Julie Ryman's mother's, or
grandmother's, or was it just an antique which had caught
her eye as she browsed through a store? A woman like her
probably did a lot of browsing in good stores that had beautiful things whose purchase might dent the boredom of a
Beverly Hills afternoon. The diamond bracelets had modern
settings but the gems themselves were of a high carat. They
had cost plenty. The wedding ring was a plain band of
reddish gold. The price of the marriage it symbolized had
cost Julie Ryman her life and might yet cost me mine.

The jewelry wasn't any good to Julie Ryman anymore but
I thought her husband might like to have it back. If anyone
knew how it had gotten from a Hollywood motel room four
days ago into the hubcap of my car, I thought it was him.

22

Ryman's car was a dark green nine-passenger Cadillac limousine, the kind Arabs and banana-republic dictators buy with their oil revenues and foreign-aid handouts. It looked like someone had cut a normal-sized car in the middle and then inserted a lounge between the two halves. It was parked in front of a concrete and chrome-fronted office building near the junction of La Cienega and Santa Monica Boulevard. A chauffeur sat behind the wheel in black sunglasses and a dark-visored cap. What you could see of his face and neck was the color of raw pork.

The car was in a NO STOPPING zone with its tail blocking a fire hydrant. Every once in a while a motorcycle cop slowly cruised by, gave it a looking over, but thought better of writing a ticket.

I was parked up the block on the other side of the street with my side mirror angled to keep it in view. Just before noon the chauffeur made a call from his radio telephone, then got out and checked that all the doors were locked. He was dressed in a black uniform with an equestrian military cut that made him look like Mussolini. The jacket was tight over his barrel chest and heavy shoulders; riding breeches flared out above his gleaming black boots. He checked his watch and then crossed over the traffic, bought a newspaper, and went into a beanery on Melrose.

I studied the office building which Ryman had gone into earlier that morning. I could just barely detect glimpses of movement behind its smoked brown windows, secretaries gliding by, the ordinary activity going on. I transferred the jewels from the glove compartment to my pocket and got out of my car. Crossing the street I was so nervous I had to force myself not to turn back. I had the impression that I was being watched by dozens of eyes and the instant I tried to plant the jewels on Ryman's car all hell would break loose. As I strolled down the pavement the Cadillac loomed closer and closer. My pulse rate was climbing. Why was I even doing this? What purpose would it serve? Maybe I should have taken the jewels to the police the second I found them? This inner argument was raging furiously as I approached the Cadillac. I'd intended to casually drop the bag into the curved well of the rear bumper but at the vital moment my nerve failed. I passed the car without stopping. I would go to the police, I thought; it was insane to walk around with damaging evidence in my pocket. Or was I just frightened, simply afraid to do what I'd set out to do? It was suddenly a point of honor. I wheeled around and walked back to the limousine, reaching my hand into my pocket.

At that moment several things happened at once. A red Facel Vega shrieked to a halt behind the Cadillac and Lisa Williams' husband jumped out. I heard footsteps running behind me, turned, and saw the chauffeur bearing down on me. The doors to the office building slid open and Ryman came hurrying down the steps.

My mind was working with an extraordinary swiftness and clarity; I saw exactly how the chauffeur's call must have alerted Ryman to my presence outside the building, how Ryman must have called Williams to come over at once. I could even imagine how lame my explanation would sound to Sunday when I tried to account for the jewels in my pocket. I understood it all in a flash but my body was paralyzed with confusion. I didn't know which way to turn. By the time I'd thought about it, the chauffeur had hold of my arm and there was something pointed and hard pressing into my ribs.

"Wait a minute," I said. "Be cool. Take it easy. Is that a gun? Is that a loaded gun? Just don't do anything stupid. Wait a minute . . ." I couldn't stop talking. "Hold it a second."

The chauffeur wasn't saying anything. He just kept dragging me along to the car where Ryman and Williams were waiting. They both looked extremely apprehensive, looking around to see if we were being observed.

"I didn't know you were friends," I said.

"Get him in the car," Ryman barked.

The chauffeur was strong but one hand was taken up with the gun and there wasn't a lot he could do with me except hang on. "Wait a minute." I kept talking to him. "This is stupid. Are you crazy? Put the gun away. Do you want to kill someone?"

Ryman grabbed my other arm and started pulling me toward the open car door. I twisted free of his grip, kicking out wildly, connecting on his kneecap. He went down with one leg under him, losing his glasses, roaring at Williams to do something. The chauffeur was braced behind me shoving me at the door but making no headway. It was all very clumsy, very confused, very unlike movie violence. Ryman kicked at me from where he was lying on the pavement and succeeded in hitting his chauffeur's ankle. Williams, who'd been holding the door open, now also got into the act. He grabbed my shirt front and tried to pull me forward in one all-out movement but the material ripped. He went crashing back against the side of the car. Throughout this scuffle I refrained from hitting the chauffeur and he refrained from hitting me. It was almost as if we'd come to an unspoken agreement. His job was to hold on to me, to push me toward the open door. So long as I didn't try and kick or punch him he wasn't going to do anything else. The other two were fair game, though, and I hit out freely at them with my one hand and got in a few kicks. It was really a remarkably undignified, inconclusive struggle, more like a shoving match between five-year-olds than anything else. When they finally got me into the backseat I climbed over the partition into the driver's seat and started to go out his door. They all rushed around so I locked his door and scrambled back and locked the door I'd come in by. They had keys of course but there were six doors to the limousine and only three of them so it was something they had to figure out. By then they were hardly in great shape for much deductive reasoning. They were all of them red in the face and furiously aware that if they didn't resolve this Laurel-and-Hardy routine pretty quickly someone would notice and call the police.

Just to keep them off balance I kept making feints at different doors while they shouted orders at each other and ran around the car. In the course of all that confusion I managed to ditch the bag of jewels in the chenille-upholstered backseat. The whole business had me so absorbed that I didn't have time to be frightened; in fact, once I'd stashed the jewels I think I was almost enjoying myself. But maybe that's not quite accurate. What I really felt, I believe, was contempt for their ineptness. There was something definitely flabby and panic-stricken in the way they were going about things, something very shabbily conceived about it all. I don't know what I expected but it certainly wasn't anything so ludicrous as the spectacle of them peering at me through the limousine windows. It had never occurred to me that evil—and they were evil men—could take such absurd form that it smacked of farce.

Glaring at me through the windows with their anxious red faces, they looked asinine and all too human. Their mouths were open and panting, clouding over the glass with mist.

In the end I just sat back in the middle of the seat and folded my arms. They paused a moment, suspecting it was a trick. Then the chauffeur got in behind the wheel and pushed a button unlocking all the doors, and Ryman and Williams got in on either side of me.

"All right, Cole." Williams gripped my arm. "We've got you."

"Yeah," Ryman wheezed. "We got him."

I couldn't think of anything appropriate to answer. There was a moment when no one said anything. They were both jammed up against me, their heated, perspiring faces a few inches from mine, both breathing heavily.

"So what's the big idea?" Ryman finally gasped.

"What are you doing here?" Williams shook my arm.

"What are *you* two doing here?" I countered. "Small world, don't you think?"

"We're asking the questions," Williams growled.

"So ask." I shrugged indifferently.

Neither of them said anything. They exchanged glances.

"We ought to take him to the police," Ryman suggested.

"How'd you like that, Cole?" Williams gave my arm another shaking.

"The police can pick me up anytime they want. Stop pawing me, for Christ's sake."

"You still haven't told us what you're doing here," Williams said.

"You know, apart from being an incredible asshole, you're very dense. What the hell do you think I'm doing here? I'm being framed for murder, thanks to both of you."

"You killed my wife," Ryman tried to snarl but it lacked a certain conviction. It was like something he'd only just now remembered.

"Whose benefit is this for?" I crossed my legs. "For Williams? Williams knows damn well I was in bed with his wife the night your wife was killed."

"We ought to search him," Ryman gasped hoarsely.

"You're right," Williams assented.

I pretended to resist and we had another scuffle but eventually I let them go through my pockets. They got my keys and told the chauffeur to go search my car. It was beginning to dawn on me that they had no intention of taking me to the police. In fact, they didn't have the faintest idea what to do with me at all.

"You're going to get the electric chair, you bastard," Ryman nodded furiously.

"We know you killed her."

They kept muttering things like that to keep up their spirits while the chauffeur was gone. At the time it just amazed me. I couldn't see why they bothered to say all these things which were so clearly untrue. They knew that I knew that they were totally and irredeemably full of shit but still they went on in that vein. Do you think they were embarrassed? They didn't need to hide the truth. There wasn't anything I could do about it. But they still maintained their stuffy, indignant front, as if they were the injured parties. I would never in a million years have been able to guess such weirdness would come out of them.

The chauffeur finally came back and reported that my car was empty.

"He could have had a gun," Williams said hollowly.

"Now I suppose we'll have to let him go. Just shows you what kind of legal system we've got. The bastard's guilty and we can't touch him." Ryman opened his door and got out and stood looking worriedly around. "Come on, Cole. Get out of there."

The chauffeur returned my car keys to me. I stepped out into the street. Ryman climbed back inside, slammed the door, and then rolled the window down a few inches.

"Next time," he rasped, "will be the last time for you. You're on borrowed time, Cole." His eyes bulged insanely behind the thick lenses; little pockets of spittle had collected in the corners of his mouth. "You're never going to do that to anyone's wife again. Never! We're going to make sure of it." The window rolled up and he slumped exhausted in the backseat next to Williams. With a smooth purr, the car accelerated from the curb and a moment later it was lost in the midday traffic.

Sometimes I get into moods where I wish I'd done something awful to both of them. Ryman still drives around Beverly Hills in his limousine and in his madder more dishonest moments probably half convinces himself that it was not him but someone else who destroyed his wife. Williams still spends his Friday nights with whatever boy Anne Laughton provides him with, and Lisa surely has another young man to escort her to auctions and service her in her upstairs study. And where am I? In an eight-by-ten cell with Calvin Potts who killed a man over a glass of spilled beer. If there is a hidden sense of justice in that it must be very well hidden. I don't see it at all.

23

I might as well admit I was pretty pleased with the way I'd handled myself with them, not to mention having entirely fooled them about the jewels. If I wasn't John Wayne, I still had more nerve and courage than I'd imagined. Now, of course, I see that all I did was play into their hands but at the time I thought I'd finally struck a blow.

My confidence, however, wasn't destined to last very long. I telephoned my hotel from a pay phone to see if there were any messages and got Wibak on the switchboard. He said Michelle had been calling all morning and there were uniformed cops waiting in the lobby and staked out on the street. They'd gone through the hotel with a fine-tooth comb and found something but he didn't know what it was. It was all very bad for business, and he was sorry but I would have to find another place to live. In mid-sentence the phone was taken from him and Sunday said, "Where are you, Cole?" whereupon I hung up.

Maybe I should have gone back to the hotel and turned myself in, but the prospect of prison was very unattractive. I had some unfinished business; it would be very convenient for certain parties were I to be safely stashed away behind bars and I didn't think I was that interested in making it easy for them.

I telephoned Anne Laughton next to see if she'd been able to come up with anything helpful on Ryman or Williams. My heart sank as I heard her voice angrily shrieking: "That does it. You were meant to pick the Swedish woman up at the airport this morning. Do you know what this has cost me? My whole reputation for reliability is shot to hell. The biggest trick on my books. A whole goddamn market depended on it . . ."

"Anne, I'm sorry. You don't know what's been happening . . ."

"Who cares? You blew it."

"Can we get together? I need your help."

"My help?" she snorted. "Let me tell you something, sweetheart. No one needs you. You've been replaced. You like to think your clients are discriminating but they really aren't. Any boy will do."

"All right, I'm expendable. Just tell me who else tricked with the Rymans."

"You don't get it yet. You're washed up. You don't work for me. You never worked for me. This conversation never took place. I don't know you." She banged the phone down.

I stood there with the receiver in my hand for a moment staring blankly at the traffic going by. I thought of the hours I'd spent practicing my Swedish, listening to tapes, speaking the responses aloud, even reading Swedish novels in the original with the aid of a dictionary. All this so that I could please this woman, amuse her, make love to her in her own language. It seemed like an enormous expenditure of care and energy for an ultimately worthless end. I was wanted for murder. What did I care if this wealthy Swedish woman had been inconvenienced? It was insane. What I'd done for a living was insane. Everything that had given my life in Los Angeles the appearance of solidity was dissolving, drifting to pieces like a mirage. Nothing had stood the test. I was alone and now they were going to lay me low. I was going to be like that naked, abject Mexican at the police station: a numbered piece of meat to be punished and despised and shut out from the light. I could feel it, this terrible fate taking shape around me. I was going to be captured and hurled into the savage nightmare world of prison; stripped of my hope and manhood, treated like a caged rat. I wanted to scream at the injustice of it. What had I done to deserve this? And why was it happening now, just when I was waking up to the real possibilities of life?

I found myself dialing Michelle's number and hating myself for being so weak. I was determined to be calm. I didn't want her to feel guilty or sorry for me. I wanted to do at least one thing I could look back on without feeling ashamed of myself.

"Thank God you got my message," she said. "Where are you?"

"There are cars going by. It doesn't matter where I am really. I just wanted to say good-bye and thank you."

"Rick talked to the D.A." She interrupted me. "You mustn't go back to your hotel. They've found the murder weapon in the trash."

"That makes sense."

"You're going to need money, Julian, and a place to hide. Tell me how I can help you."

"It's all taken care of," I said. "I just want you to know that this is a frame. I never killed that woman. You have to believe that."

"Of course I do!" she cried. "I've never doubted you for a second."

It sounded strange when she said it; everyone else I knew either believed me guilty, or was dead set on proving me so whether it was true or not.

"When can I see you?" she asked.

I don't recall exactly what I told her but the gist of it was that I wasn't going to drag her into this mess. She was the one good thing that had come out of it, the one thing in my life I hadn't managed to destroy and I didn't want to start now. In any case, it was some very noble sentiment which didn't correspond at all to what I really wanted. After I'd finished my piece, she went off the deep end.

"Are you crazy?" she wailed. "I love you. You can't push me away now."

I reminded her that she was the one who was going away to Rome and it was she who had the husband whose career she couldn't endanger. I said it gently enough but it was a sore point. When she'd told me about her decision to leave Los Angeles it had really crushed me and the disappointment was still coloring my feelings for her.

"I'm not going to Rome, you fool," she insisted. "I only said I'd go so Rick would help you. That's why I kept asking if you'd wait for me. But Rick fooled me. He never intended to help you. Even if you go to prison, I'm divorcing him."

"You're just saying that."

"You would never have accepted help if you thought it was coming through Rick. But he was the only one I knew who had the power to do something. I had to lie to you, Julian."

There was a long silence while I digested what she'd said. Maybe she was right, maybe not, but I was so relieved that I was still important to her I didn't care. My resolve weakened. I shouldn't have agreed to a meeting but I knew it would be the last one and I wanted her terribly. Time was running out. I suddenly couldn't stand not to see her again.

We agreed to meet at a hotel on Pico Boulevard near the beach in two hours.

24

A black and white police car was double-parked next to my Mercedes, with its red light flashing. The officer behind the wheel was making a radio call. I turned around, crossed over the traffic, and cut through a gas station on to Melrose. Sunday must have sent out my description and the make and license number of my car to the mobile units in West Los Angeles.

As I walked down Melrose two more police cars turned off San Vicente and roared north toward Santa Monica Boulevard. A moment later I heard the whirring beat of a helicopter descending as it started a low-level sweep of the area. My eyes swept over the pedestrians I passed. None of them had black hair and blue eyes, nor were any of them my height or age. The next patrol car to cruise by would have little trouble in picking me out.

It had happened so fast it took me off guard. I'd counted on having more time before things got to this stage.

Panic is the mother of invention. At the next newspaper vending machine I passed, I put in fifteen cents and scooped out an armful of copies of that day's L.A. *Times*. I stepped into an alleyway lined with garbage cans where I found a broken straw hat. I stuck it on the back of my head and stripped off my shirt and rolled up my trousers above my knees. With the load of newspapers, the battered straw hat, and the casually worn clothes I hoped I looked like some overgrown slightly retarded newsboy.

I felt a little safer when I reached Fairfax Avenue because the pavements were considerably more crowded and the traffic heavier. I purchased a pair of fifty-cent sunglasses in Thriftys' and one of those flimsy disposable raincoats that fold up into a small bag. The sunglasses had feeble red frames, the raincoat fit me like a tent and looked extremely eccentric above my bare legs and sockless feet. In the parking lot behind the store I traded in my newspapers for some dirty looking shopping bags filled with throwaway garbage. I scooped up dust and dirt and rubbed my face and legs and chest. I was starting to look like a ragpicker, the kind who jealously guards his useless collections of refuse.

The disguise must have been good because people avoided my eyes and gave me a wide berth on the pavement. I stood out like a sore thumb but I was so unattractive and deranged looking no one gave me a second glance. I altered my walk into a splay-footed shuffle, and talked to myself as I shambled along.

When I reached Pico I caught a bus to the beach. Needless to say, with twitching and talking aloud, I had the whole backseat to myself all the way.

It worried me a little how good I was at it, and how naturally I projected myself into the role of an unbalanced young derelict. It's hard to describe my feelings but there was almost a kind of relief and perverse rightness about it. I *was* a social outcast. I *was* perhaps more than a little crazy from the strain of the last week. It was Julian Cole, the successful gigolo who now seemed to be the travesty, not the sadly ruined character I was impersonating.

I made my way across the beach through the sunbathers almost to the edge of the water where I lay down in a drifted hollow of sand. It was after four and people were starting to pack up their things to leave. The light had moved from the overpowering glare of noon into the richer softer colors of late afternoon. The sea was marbled green and white beyond the surf line and then gradually turned bluer as it extended from the shore until it was dark violet at its outer limits. A few elongated wisps of cloud were visible over the horizon, soft as smoke. Lying in the warm sand, with the sky overhead and the sea wind on my face I felt for a moment that it would be enough to be permitted to remain there for the rest of my life. I wanted nothing more than the ocean and this sense of unbounded space. I was finding out too late that I lived in a beautiful world.

After awhile I walked to the edge of the sea and washed myself. The cool saltwater was almost voluptuous on my hands and face, or maybe my senses were heightened to a pitch by the knowledge that soon all this might be taken away from me. I don't know if I was in a state of grace, or just bent out of shape by fear and uncertainty. I know I stood there gazing into space while the sun dried me and the voices of children rang above the crashing surf, and felt again that I'd missed my chance at life. I'd looked for it in the bodies of strangers, in the brittle indolence of the rich, in bedrooms and country clubs, in the bright lights of the city. I'd craved social standing, sought to be admired for my elegance and cultivation. The surf seethed around my ankles, sucking the sand from beneath my feet. There wasn't any point in lying to myself anymore. It was precisely because it was hollow that my life had disintegrated so completely. I'd lived superficially, insincerely. I'd exploited my sexuality for what were really pretty indistinguished ends. If I ever got a second chance I would go at things differently and make my mark another way. But at least, I thought, it was my own tragedy; I hadn't asked anyone to bear the cost of my mistakes. It seemed strange that only now, with my life hopelessly smashed to pieces and nothing but darkness ahead, I should finally have arrived at a knowledge of who I was.

25

Michelle had registered at the Santa Monica Inn under the name of Mrs. J. Sorel, taking a room on the fourth floor. There was a narrow ornamental balcony with a view of the ocean and a sea breeze was blowing through the terrace doors. Lying at the front of the bed were two large red leather suitcases that looked fully packed. She shut the door behind me, turned the key in the lock, and fell into my arms. I wanted her so badly I could hardly wait to get out of my clothes or undress her. I couldn't speak because my mouth would not stop finding hers and kissing it. We tumbled backward onto the bed and made love with a kind of violent urgency. At one point I remember opening my eyes and seeing the curtains stirred by the breeze and the late afternoon sky framed by the terrace doors. The room was airy and light, the bed soft. I was taken up with this warm living being, joined to her in a sensual ecstasy. Outside the walls of the room, outside the heated embrace of her body was nothing but danger and fear. I felt like Nero fiddling while Rome burned and wondered if I would remember this last, stolen hour in a hotel room overlooking the sea as the happiest of my life. I should have been making efforts to avert disaster and instead I was acting as if I had my whole life before me.

Was it because I wanted to get caught? Had I already given up hope of escaping? I find it hard to explain even now but a strange kind of peace filled me. I must have already known what I was going to do and the knowledge and acceptance of it freed me from further cares.

She had given me her love, strengthened me with it. I was now going to return it to her in the only way I knew how.

"Julian," she said afterward. "What are we going to do?"

"We're not doing anything. I wanted to see you one last time. After this I'm on my own. If you really love me, then do what I say. As soon as it's dark I'm leaving and you're going home."

Of course she didn't want to do that at all. She'd packed her suitcases with clothes for both of us and withdrawn several thousand dollars in cash. Her Alfa-Romeo was parked outside with a full tank of gas. She had come on the understanding that we would make a run for it. If I was going to prison, she said, she was going too. No sacrifice was too great for her to make if it gave us time together. She kept talking about her mother and father in wartime Paris and how her mother had tried to save her father from the Gestapo. It took all my self-control to resist her. This incredibly beautiful woman loved me enough to destroy her future for me. She knew the odds were strongly against us getting far; if she were apprehended in my company, she would face serious charges for which she'd be sent to prison. How could I take advantage of such generosity? I'd risked nothing for her. The more attractive and valuable she seemed to me, the more determined I became not to involve her. The old Julian Cole would have exploited her.

"If you go without me," she said, "I'll call the police and

tell them that I've been with you. I will confess everything and they will have to send me to prison."

"Stop this craziness."

"I don't care." She shook her head. "I'm going to kill myself anyway. You don't believe me? I have enough pills in my suitcase to do it ten times over. I know you, Julian. You're going to do something stupid. I can feel it. You're going to try and get back at these people who are doing this to you and they will kill you, or the police will kill you." Her fingers were digging into my shoulders and she was shaking and kissing me. "Where are you going?" she cried. "You must tell me."

So I invented a story that involved a friend with a yacht who was leaving that night for Oregon. I was going to board the boat as soon as it got dark. I would stay on the boat for several weeks until the heat cooled down, then fly from Portland to New York. In New York I had friends who would arrange a new identity. With another passport I would go to Europe, probably to Paris or Madrid. From there I would have to see. In any case, I went on, to travel with her would only increase my chances of being caught. Her disappearance would be immediately linked to my flight. As the wife of an American senator she would draw an enormous amount of publicity.

We made love again, and then again, and once more resumed the argument, saying the same things and coming to no agreement. The room had grown dark. The sound of traffic floated up from the street with the distant crash of the surf. We lay on our backs in silence. After awhile she slipped from the bed, rummaged for something in her luggage and went into the bathroom. I heard the key turn in the lock. It was a good time, while she was out of the room, to get dressed. I pulled on my clothes quickly in the dark, listening for some noise from the bathroom but hearing nothing. What was she doing in there? Was she reckless and proud enough to do something crazy like swallow a bottle of sleeping pills? I heard the light switch go off, the key turn in the lock, and then the door opened and she came toward me in the dark. I was sitting on the edge of the bed. She kneeled at my feet and gasped lightly when instead of feeling my bare skin she touched my clothes. She laid her face in my lap and took my hands and pressed them against her head. I stroked her and felt her thick hair in my hands.

"Now no one will recognize me," she said fiercely.

"Oh, God!" I turned on the bedside lamp and stared at her in horror. She had lopped her hair off. A thick sheaf of dark blond hair almost two feet long was in my hands. She'd hacked the rest of her hair to within a few inches of her scalp. It gave her a nutty, pleading boyish look.

At that point I had to relent. I knew she was capable of doing anything unless I held out the hope of our meeting again. I swore I'd phone her as soon as the boat docked in Oregon and then make arrangements to meet her in New York. After heated protests I accepted a thousand dollars from her in one-hundred-dollar bills.

"If you're lying to me," she said, "I'll find you and kill you."

That was the kind of crazy thing she was saying. She was really in a passion. I think if I'd suggested we commit suicide right then and there she wouldn't have hesitated. I hated lying to Michelle. I would have given anything to stay with her but going was the only way I could demonstrate I cared about her. It wasn't that I doubted her feelings but I knew they were the product of extraordinary events. I didn't want her destruction on my conscience.

When she started to cry and cling to me I pretended to be annoyed.

"Don't be so weak. Do you want the boat to go without me? How can I count on you if you're falling to pieces already?"

"You're right." She pressed herself against me. "You'll see, in New York I'll do everything. I'm crying because you've made me so happy. From now on I live only for you."

I pulled her hands from my neck, kissed them, and got out the door. I walked down the corridor to the emergency stairs and then started running down the steps. I had to get away before my resolve weakened. Already the image of her with her blond hair cropped like a nun's and her eyes wide with suffering was torturing me.

26

I'd planned on catching a bus inland from the beach but instead found myself walking. I passed banks, lit-up pawn shops, animal hospitals, liquor stores, mortuaries, hamburger joints, cinemas. It was like moving through a tunnel of neon. The miles unrolled. In the distance the colors grew blurred; the boulevard extended straight and true like a brightly burning filament into the heart of the night.

I needed sleep and food, I was sure, but my body didn't seem to want them. I didn't walk fast but I kept up a steady pace that slowly ate up the miles. The monotony of it emptied my mind. I didn't think any more of Michelle. The odd police cars I saw cruising the boulevard set off no alarm bells of fear. It was as if a magnet out there in the night was controlling my speed and direction, inexorably drawing me to itself. And I was calm almost to the point of resignation. Nothing excited me anymore. Nothing frightened me. Nothing was going to stop me.

The night grew cool, and a damp fog began blowing in from the beach, wetting the streets and misting the lights of the city. By the time I reached Westwood it was after midnight and the traffic was sparse so that you heard each individual car approaching out of the fog. Near Rancho Park the air changed from the proximity of the golf course and playing fields, becoming sweet with the humid earth-smell of wet grass and trees. Up ahead, like dimly blazing rectangles of light, the Century City skyscrapers loomed in the fog. At the sight of them a trace of anger stirred in me. I shivered in my clothes and felt for the first time how bone-tired and played-out I was.

I carried on past the Twentieth Century-Fox Studios. Inside the wire-enclosed lot the deserted plywood stage sets of old city streets and western saloon fronts were brilliantly spot-lit. Seen from the front they had the appearance of reality. From the side they revealed themselves as cunningly constructed illusions. The same spirit of imitation that had motivated the movie industry had colored the building of the rest of the city. The surrounding residential streets were lined with flimsy stucco fantasies of English cottages and Moorish castles, French chateaux and Elizabethan manors, as unreal in the misty light as the abandoned stage sets.

I turned north on Avenue of the Stars and approached the vast illuminated monoliths of Century City office buildings and apartment towers. On their tops were helicopter landing-pads and tennis courts; below, at street level, shopping malls honeycombed with beauty parlors, health clubs, and restaurants, and below that, subterranean levels of parking lots. After awhile I stepped off the pavement and crossed a bleakly landscaped stretch of ground that dipped down toward a glittering apartment tower. The grass was soggy underfoot, sparsely planted at intervals with baby trees and potted shrubs. Their meager presence only seemed to enhance the man-made emptiness of the place.

A driveway swept in a half circle around the front of the building where a few cars were parked and a doorman in livery was on duty. Through the lobby windows I could see a fountain bubbling colored water into a tiled pool. I made my way around to the back of the building where the garage entrance was, and set myself to wait in the bushes.

A fine rain began falling like the delicate mist of an atomizer. It felt cold for late August.

After a few moments the headlights of a car swept across the shrubs and a white Fleetwood sighed to a stop in front of the garage doors. The side window purred down, a hand emerged from inside and fitted a key into the remote-control lock, activating the gate to open. I waited until the car had vanished down the ramp and then stepped inside as the gates closed behind me.

There were two parking levels connected by escalators. I found Leroy's Continental parked in the lower one. His full name, Leroy Roosevelt Cleveland, was stenciled to the cement wall, with his apartment number beneath it. His radio-telephone antennae had been replaced but looking through the windows I saw an empty gap where the telephone was meant to be. The hood was cool to the touch. I kneeled down and let the air out of all four tires. On my way to the elevator I passed the zone for guest parking and noticed an early model brown Porsche. I was sure it was the car driven by the blond man I'd seen in my hotel garage. I deflated his tires, too.

Had I already lost my head at that point? Was I already premeditating what was going to happen? The District Attorney would like to believe so. I'm not sure myself. I think I'd come to confront my fate. Not with much hope of changing it but at least to stare it in the face and call it by its real name. I couldn't stand the idea of being destroyed invisibly from a distance any longer.

I stood outside Leroy's apartment door on the twelfth

floor and listened. I could faintly hear Dylan's "Sad Eyed Lady of the Lowlands" and a man's svelte baritone laughter coming from inside. My heart was beating so hard it hurt and I had a terrible ringing pain in my temples. I knocked twice sharply.

The music stopped and there was a long silence. I knocked again. I heard a door opening, footsteps, and then Leroy's voice on the other side of the door.

"Who's that?"

"It's Julian. Let me in, it's important."

There was a pause and then the door opened and Leroy stepped back to let me past. It was almost the only time I'd seen him unable to maintain his deadpan expression. His eyes were wide with astonishment, his forehead wrinkled in apprehension, his mouth hung open a little. It only lasted a second and then the mask hardened and the cold mocking grin formed on his lips.

"Julie, you look terrible. You want to clean up? Get a shave?" He cocked his head and arched one eyebrow, making a pawing gesture in the air with his limp-wristed hand. He was dressed in a shiny silver outfit that was meant to be a sort of chic astronaut's suit, with lots of zippers and colored decals on the arms and chest. It was very tight and crackled like silver foil when he moved.

"You look great, Leroy." I followed the corridor into the living room. "When are they sending you to the moon?"

As I stepped into the living room I saw the blond boy slip into the bedroom and silently shut the door. I glanced around. The place was done up in contemporary chrome and glass, with white leather sofas and chairs, and framed Andy Warhol lithographs on the white walls. There were three elongated steel lamps with chrome shades that looked like inserts bending over the Plexiglas tables. Everything was cold, white, hard, and geometrically arranged. The room was decorated with that ruthless lack of color and sensual form that passes for good taste among people who are frightened of any display of beauty.

A small hand mirror lay on the Plexiglas table, with several fat lines of brown cocaine laid out on it. Beside it was a chrome cutthroat razor with a white bone handle and a silver straw for sniffing the drug. The razor gave off a dazzling bluish radiance under the lights.

Leroy stepped into the room, his eyes flitting to the table and to the closed bedroom door. "You want to get high?" he said.

"I'm here for my alibi."

"It's not ready yet." He sat down and bent over the coke, straightening a line with the edge of the razor. "But I'm working on it. It ain't that easy, you know."

I sat on the edge of a chair opposite him and watched as he inserted the silver straw into his right nostril, pinched the left shut with his forefinger, and bent to the mirror. I let out my breath in a powerful blast, blowing the coke away.

"What the fuck . . ." he gasped.

"Why are you framing me, Leroy?"

"You crazy, man?" He glared at me in alarm. "No one's framing you. I'm getting you off like you asked me. You think this shit grows on trees? That's fifty dollars you just wasted."

"You can afford it, with what they're paying you."

His face was twisted into a grimace of indignation. "I can't believe how uncool you are, Julie. The man's gonna call any time 'bout your alibi."

I stood up and took a turn around the room. The balcony doors were open and I could see rain falling on the gleaming wet tiles of the terrace. It was a real rain now, coming down hard. When I resumed my seat I noticed that the razor was no longer on the table. Leroy looked at me with a hurt, faintly puzzled expression as if he'd been unfairly treated. For some reason this annoyed me more than anything. They must have thought I was incredibly stupid, I thought to myself, to swallow it in the first place.

"Your boyfriend's awfully shy," I said conversationally.

"He don't feel so good."

"Maybe you're working him too hard, Leroy. Planting all that evidence in my room and car must have worn him out."

"You are one paranoid motherfucker." Leroy rolled his eyeballs and sighed in exasperation. "I'm the one person trying to help you and all you do is make these offhand accusations. I don't know where you get all this jive from, man. You're just biting the hand that feeds you."

"He's the one that actually killed her, isn't he?" I said calmly. "Got into a scene with Ryman and his wife. Got a little rough and killed her. Then you had to get someone to take the fall. It couldn't be the boy, couldn't be Ryman, so . . ."

"I've been worked over three times by the police on this case," he sneered. "Ask them if I'm clean or not."

"Just answer me one question: how much do I have to pay to get off the hook?"

"Who's talking about money? You want an alibi, I'm providing it. I didn't ask you for no money."

"How much?" I smiled at him, my sleaziest grimace. "Just the figure?"

"I'll tell you." He turned sideways and looked at me over his shoulder, the hatred hovering just below the surface of his chiseled black face. "It don't matter how much, Julie. The other side will always pay more."

"You got the frame on pretty tight, don't you, Leroy?"

He shrugged, not looking at me, as if I bored him, as if I was already among the marks and losers. "Ryman's chauffeur found those jewels you planted," he said. "Took them right to the police and told them what happened. That's three witnesses right there. They found the murder weapon in the trash at your hotel. I don't know what you're thinking about coming here, man. I don't harbor fugitives." He stood up and went and leaned against the mantel in a casual attitude. He seemed to be waiting for something, listening alertly. Had the blond boy gone into the bedroom to phone the police? "It's all over." He glanced at me with flat, pitiless eyes. "You have become like a drag, man."

As I got to my feet, he made a jiggling motion with his wrist and the razor slipped out of his sleeve into his palm. He flicked out the blade and held it out high and straight as if it were a glass and he was toasting me. In his black hand the blade had a dazzling brilliance. He turned it in the light, making it sparkle, showing it to me.

"You already done a lot of stupid things," he said softly. "You want to try for one more?"

"Why me, Leroy?" I asked. "Why did you pick me to frame?"

"Because you were framable, baby. You stepped on too many toes. Nobody cared about you." He paused and then said, "I never liked you much anyway. You ain't hip to what kind of business you're in. You thought you were selling love and kindness to them bitches. . . ."

As he talked I measured the distance between us, and watched the blade. We were separated by the low Plexiglas table whose edge rested against my shin.

"I ain't in the therapy business," he scoffed. "I'm a packager. I package meat. I ain't got no use for uppity dudes who want to pick and choose their tricks. . . ."

I made a sudden lifting movement, kicking the table up at his face. He seemed to have all the time in the world to knock it aside with his arm. I wasn't prepared for a counterattack and saw nothing but a blur as he struck home. My cheek burned, opened to the bone by one slash of the razor. He backed around into the open space of the living room while I turned to keep him in view, holding my face. The blood was pouring through my fingers, dripping to the white carpet. I could feel the side of my face pulsing, aching, the warmth running down my neck and chest. Waves of shock and nausea swept through me.

"You gonna try for two?" Leroy waggled the blade suggestively. "You wanna turn the other cheek, white boy?"

He was crouched low, with both hands out, his back to the open terrace doors. I remember grabbing one of the lamps, ripping its cord from the socket, and swinging its heavy metal base at him. I remember his scream of pain as it cracked against the arm he had raised to defend himself. Behind me I heard the bedroom door open, and saw the blond boy out of the corner of my eye running out of the living room. Leroy was trying to slam the terrace doors closed but I jabbed the lamp at his face and he had to jump back.

He retreated to the far end of the terrace, crouching, with the razor held at the ready and his other hand to his mouth. I couldn't see his face clearly, only his razor and the fluorescent gleam of his astronaut suit. For a moment we both stood there, panting, with the rain drumming on the slippery tiles. I picked up a flowerpot and hurled it at his head and missed. It sailed off into the blackness and a moment later I heard it explode with a distant crack on the pavement. I grabbed another one and threw it, losing my footing on the treacherously wet tiles. He charged me, hacking out with the blade. I was on my back, kicking up at him, taking his blows on my shoes. The razor came flashing down at my face and I raised my arm to ward it off and felt it burn my wrist.

From then on, I'm not clear. I remember my foot kicking and landing against something solid that could have been his face, and the sharp clatter of the razor hitting the tiles. I remember his hand around my throat and his hot breath in my face. We struggled to our feet, wrestling. He bit my chest and I screamed at the pain and horror of it. My feet slipped again just as he was pushing me to the railing, and his own momentum carried him over the edge. I caught his leg and held on. For an instant he was hanging backwards, one leg hooked over the balcony, the rest of his body splayed out in empty space. His wallet and change slipped from his pockets, falling into the rainy blackness. He made a violent heaving effort to arch himself back up but I was losing my grip. The razor slash had lamed my right wrist. The leg I was holding on to with my left hand started to slip until I was holding his shoe by the ankle and then the weight of his body pulled him free. He was a blur of radiant silver plummeting into the blackness that swallowed him from view and gave back a horrific noise as he hit the pavement.

A few moments after the thud of his body striking the concrete, I heard sirens wailing on Avenue of the Stars, followed by the squeal of tires, and car doors slamming. Voices and radio static drifted up. Flashes of red light from the police cars faintly stained the mist swirling around the terrace. I remember lying curled up on the wet tiles, clutching something to my stomach which must have been Leroy's shoe. The cold rain was slanting down into my face. I could feel the drops striking but I couldn't see them. My cheek and wrist tingled with a weak burning warmth. Before I passed out from loss of blood I heard distant bangings and voices which must have been the police breaking down Leroy's door.

27

The pale green visitors' room is high and long and too brightly illuminated. On her side and my side of the plate glass panel the prison guards stand with dull, fixed expressions on their faces. You cannot do anything through the glass except look at the person opposite you. You are allowed to speak but you must use the telephones which rest in front of you. It feels endlessly strange and cruel to be talking on the phone to someone whose face is a foot away from yours, but that is how it's done, as if we, the prisoners, have a disease which might be infectious to our visitors.

I know I must be shocking Michelle by my appearance. I can see my face reflected in the plate glass panel and it has already turned pasty from the prison diet and lack of sunlight. Because of the dressing on my cheek I've been given permission to let my beard grow.

I can see she has dressed with care, and consciously avoided anything glamorous or provocative in her clothes or makeup in case it upsets me, and so I will know she considers herself in mourning. She wants to know why I've refused to see her, or any of the lawyers she has hired on my behalf. But I find I can't explain my behavior. There is no way to put into words the depth of resignation I feel, a resignation which the prison instills and confirms unrelentingly. It is as if I am buried at the bottom of a pale green tank, with the weight of the water pressing into every square inch of my body so that I can only move slowly. This great pressure of gloom makes quickness or brightness of thought impossible. It takes all my concentration to just maintain the illusion that I'm awake and alive like other men.

Sitting opposite me, her eyes animated by emotion, her voice full of strength and energy, Michelle seems like a stranger who belongs to another order of reality. She exists on light, sunshine, fresh air. She believes in a future and is nourished by hope. She tires me. Her emotions tire me, she is such a naturally bright spirit. I feel like she is trying to bring me back from the dead, willing me back to life but the effort is too great for me. I might as well be lying paralyzed in an iron lung dimly aware of something beating on the observation panel.

She begins to cry, but when I reach out to her my fingers touch only glass. It is not real glass but some kind of clear plastic which has gone slightly cloudy with time. All over its surface are minute hairline scratches where fingernails have grazed its surface when instinct prompted a prisoner to reach out for a loved one. It must have happened thousands of times and always with the same result. The futility of it makes me shake my head. She is staring at me wide-eyed with distress. A hairdresser has tried to put right the rough job she did to her hair but he could only try and even it up. It is cut very short like a helmet with a straight fringe and sharp points by the ears. She looks younger and more gamin than I remember. But even the sight of her face, wracked by love and suffering, doesn't affect me as it should. A great ugliness has descended on me like a dark night of the soul. I can think of nothing but the prison, the police, and the people who put me here. In the face of that, love seems absurd. It is as if love isn't strong enough to defend itself against the world. There is probably an awful lot of self-pity at work in me and beneath that a great sense of disillusionment, for I find I have nothing left to believe in except the unanswerable power of injustice. I think I'd rather believe in nothing than that.

I see the guard on her side of the plastic panel look up at the clock on the wall and check it against his wrist watch. Any moment now he will walk the length of the communication booths and dispassionately inform the Senator's wife that her visiting period is up.

"It's no good loving me," I hear my voice speaking. "I did kill Leroy. I confessed it."

"It was self-defense."

"At the best they might drop it to manslaughter. Does it really matter? They believe I killed Julie Ryman and the one person who could prove I didn't is dead."

"Do you remember the night Julie Ryman was killed?" Her eyes are bright with a keen resolute fire. "Do you remember what you did?"

"I went out with Lisa Williams."

"No you didn't. You've lied all this time to protect me." She lowers her voice. "I can't let you do it anymore. I would have told the police sooner but I was afraid of hurting my husband's reputation."

"What are you . . . ?"

"We made love that night." Her lips softened in a smile.

"You're just making it harder, Michelle."

"We made love," she insists. "Many times. Far into the

night. And because you loved me you lied to the police. You cared about my reputation more than your own safety."

"You know that's not true."

"It is more of a truth and there is more justice in it than what they are doing to you," she whispers fiercely.

"I don't want you to do this."

"It's already done," she says. "I gave my testimony to the District Attorney this morning. I had the numbers of the hundred-dollar-bills which they found on you. I confessed to helping you. Miss Breame even says I was there that night— at least she thinks I may have been there. She's not sure because I was there so many times. There is no case against you anymore."

"And Leroy?" I am too astounded to grasp it all yet.

"You'll have the best lawyers in Los Angeles. You'll be in court with a terrible scar on your face. Leroy was a known procurer and drug dealer. You were defending yourself. Once you're cleared of the Ryman murder it proves that there really was a frame against you."

The guard hitches up his belt and begins the slow walk toward her. Behind me I can hear my guard approaching, the squeak of his rubber soles over the linoleum, the jingle of his keys and handcuffs.

"Don't despair," she says. "I love you, Julian. . . ." They are the last words I hear for she replaces the receiver and rises just as the guard reaches her. Against my ear the phone gives off nothing but a low hum.

"Time's up." My guard's hand falls lightly on my shoulder and stays there until I stand up. I keep my head twisted around as he escorts me from the hall, holding her in sight until she passes through the swinging doors. My hand rises to my cheek and wonderingly touches the plaster covering the wound. Tomorrow the stitches will come out. The scar will never go away. It will be red and livid for some time but eventually I hope it will fade and turn white. The sunshine will heal and bleach it—the sunshine beyond these walls which one day will warm both of us.